Fighting Gravity

A Red-Carpet Romance

Baxter Redman

Wandering Quill Press

ISBN 978-1-971692-00-5 (paperback)
ISBN 978-1-971692-01-2 (ebook)

Published by Wandering Quill Press

For Wendy... Thanks for always cheering me on.

Chapter One

♥

East Lansing, Michigan
Red Carpet Premiere of **Fighting Gravity**

Jace Rose adjusted the cuff of his tuxedo jacket for the third time in as many minutes. The flashes were blinding. The questions never changed—how did he feel about the film? What was it like stepping back into the spotlight to record the title track? Was a full-length album next? When would Inferno tour again?

He smiled, nodded, offered the answers he was supposed to give—and hoped they landed.

This wasn't supposed to be his night. It was about the film. About his biggest fans: his mother and sister, the ones who'd convinced him to step into the booth one more time.

When he told Heather he'd been asked to record the theme song for *Fighting Gravity*, she'd squealed louder than an arena full of teenage girls.

"And you're gonna do it, right, Jace? I know you've said you don't want to perform anymore, but this book—"

She'd clutched her chest, closed her eyes, and sighed so deeply he half-wondered if she might pass out.

"It's life-changing. Seriously life-changing. You *have* to do this. I'll never speak to you again if you pass it up."

"And that would be bad how?" he'd teased.

But the truth was, he'd already made up his mind. There were only two people in the world he'd do anything for—and they rarely asked for anything. So when his mom and sister both said *please*, he didn't say no.

He recorded the love song without cracking the book. Figured it was a good gig. A meaningful one. But still just a gig.

He never expected it to blow up—or to put him right back in the spotlight. Yet here he was, standing between Carol Anne and Heather, all three of them dressed to the nines, smiling for the cameras. And wishing, if he were honest, that he was anywhere else.

Then he heard it.

Laughter.

Not polite. Not forced. Real. Sparkling.

He glanced across the red carpet and—bam.

There she was.

The woman in the emerald green gown.

Her hair fell in auburn waves, half-pinned to reveal the graceful curve of her neck. She moved with ease, elegance in every step—but not the kind that screamed *trained red carpet pro*. No, this was something else. Something grounded. She didn't just walk into a room—she *commanded* it.

The photographers were shouting—"Spencer! Over here!"—and she turned mid-laugh, reacting to something Jake Gyllenhaal had said.

And Jace's world tilted.

No way.

That's Spencer Callahan?

He blinked. Swallowed. Took half a step forward before his mother's hand on his arm gently stopped him.

"You're staring," she whispered.

"I just... I thought Spencer was—"

"A man?" his mother said with a knowing grin. "You and everyone else. Maybe next time, read the book before you sing the theme song."

Jace chuckled, still a little dazed. He leaned closer and murmured, "What's this movie even about, anyway?"

Carol Anne laughed and patted his arm. "Sweetheart, you really should do your homework. It's about survival. Resilience. Life. The story's more you than you realize."

And suddenly, it wasn't just a gig. Or a movie.

It was *her* story.

And for the first time all night, Jace didn't want to be anywhere else.

□□□

Spencer Callahan stood just left of center on the carpet, trying desperately to maintain an air of poised elegance while her heart pounded like a marching band on Red Bull.

Her movie.

Her breakout book turned full-blown cinematic experience.

Amy Adams in the lead. Jake Gyllenhaal playing her emotionally tormented dreamboat.

The whole night was surreal.

But not as surreal as the soundtrack.

That's what got her.

Every. Single. Time.

She'd heard the theme song dozens of times—had ugly-cried through it more than once—and she still couldn't believe it was real. That voice. Jace Rose. Singing the lyrics she'd written.

Well... *some* of her lyrics.

They'd been changed before the final recording. She didn't know who had rewritten them, and if the changes hadn't been so *eerily perfect*, she might have been upset. She'd written words that matched the tone of the story. But what Jace sang...

Those lyrics had no right to fit as perfectly as they did.

No one who hadn't *lived it* should've been able to capture it like that—or set it to a melody that lasted just over four and a half minutes. And yet somehow, through the ache in his voice and the raw honesty in those altered lyrics, Jace Rose made her believe he'd been there.

Made her *feel* like he had.

She only wished the studio had convinced him to perform it live tonight. But he'd declined. Said he wasn't interested in performing in public.

Assuming that meant he wouldn't be at the premiere, Spencer had tried to let it go. Meeting Jace Rose wouldn't make the night more magical. She was already living the dream. Thirty years old, five novels published, and the one that mattered most—the most *personal*—had been seen by the world. Picked up by a major studio. Adapted into what was already being called the most anticipated film of the year.

She didn't need to meet the pop star whose face had covered her bedroom walls from ages fourteen to twenty-two.

Even if that face *had* inspired the heartthrob in her book.

"Spencer! Over here!"

On her right, Jake Gyllenhaal leaned in and whispered, "I think they want your picture."

Spencer laughed—probably louder than necessary. Seven years of writing under a pen name, and she still wasn't used to hearing it aloud in public. On forums, sure. But in real life, no one called her Spencer. Or Ms. Callahan. She was just Angie Smith, small-town girl from Eaton Rapids who happened to have a knack for storytelling.

The laughter was still on her lips as she turned toward the cameras. And her heart stopped.

Just beyond the flashbulbs, standing like he'd stepped out of *GQ*, was Jace Rose.

Spencer's smile froze, and she forgot how to breathe.

He was looking at her. *Smiling* at her.

Jace. Freaking. Rose. Was. Smiling.

At. Her.

"Is this really happening?" she whisper-laughed.

"Of course it is," Jake said beside her, still posing with practiced ease.

Amy Adams, radiant as ever, stood on her other side. "It's happening because of you," she said, gently squeezing Spencer's arm. "You made this moment possible. And girl, you look damn good doing it."

Chapter Two

♥

Wharton Gardens – Premiere Afterparty

Evening breeze. Soft lighting. A jazz quartet playing low and slow.

Jace moved through the crowd like he had at hundreds of red carpet events, hundreds of afterparties—except tonight felt different.

Maybe it was the film.

Maybe it was the fact that, for once, he wasn't the center of attention.

Or maybe it was her.

He hadn't expected much going in. Figured it was a soft, swoony love story—sweet, sentimental fluff. That's what the song had led him to believe.

But then the lights dimmed, and the story began...

He fought to breathe. Forgot to blink. From the opening frame—an ivy-covered tool shed, weathered picket fence, rose bushes blooming against the edge of the screen—Jace was completely, devastatingly hooked.

Not because the acting was phenomenal, though it was.

Not because the script was sharp, layered, and nuanced, though it absolutely was.

But because it felt real. Deep. Raw.

It wasn't just a love story.

Not really.

It was about survival. About reclaiming your voice after it had been stolen. About trust. Pain. Healing. And the aching hope that maybe—just maybe—love could be part of that healing too.

He hadn't blinked through the final scenes.

And now?

He couldn't not talk to her.

He spotted her near the edge of the terrace, luminous in the golden glow of the string lights. The emerald gown shimmered around her like it had been woven from moonlight and magic. In one hand, she held a half-empty champagne flute. In the other? A glittering clutch that probably held what was left of his emotional stability.

Spencer Callahan.

Did she have any idea what she'd done to him with her story?

Jace grabbed two fresh glasses of champagne from a passing tray, took a breath, and crossed the floor.

□□□

She saw him.

Spencer was mid-conversation with Zach Braff, who had brought her story to life in ways she still couldn't believe. He was asking about the climactic scene—the one where Max tells Cassie she's in his heart, and that if she ever can't find herself, he'll pull the pieces from inside *him* to build her back into the strong woman he knows she can be.

But Spencer wasn't hearing him anymore.

Because over Zach's shoulder, under twinkling lights, she saw him.

Jace Rose.

Walking toward her.

Two glasses of champagne in hand.

Looking like something out of a cologne ad.

And coming straight for her.

Can this be true?

Is it real?

Jace Rose—smiling that ridiculous, megawatt smile—headed in her direction.

Her heart stuttered. Then skipped. Then did some kind of weird Irish tap dance that absolutely wasn't medically sound.

Why now?

Why not during the screening, when her stomach was in knots and she was convinced Roger Ebert's ghost would rise from the grave and declare her the death of modern cinema?

But now?

The movie was over.

The crowd had loved it.

Critics were nodding.

She was glowing with success and disbelief and something dangerously close to joy.

So why did the panic wait until *now* to set in?

□□□

He was ten feet away when she glanced in his direction—just for a second, just long enough for Jace to register that her eyes were the same shade of emerald as her dress—before she turned quickly, distracted by a woman with a microphone and a no-nonsense stride.

Wendy Rakowski. People Magazine.

Jace remembered her from the Inferno days. Wendy didn't take no for an answer. If she wanted an interview, she got it. And if she didn't get exactly what she wanted—but sensed there was more—she had no problem twisting the facts until they lined up with the headline she'd already written.

With a smile, Jace paused. Still holding both champagne flutes, he backed off just slightly, giving them space. He didn't want to interrupt. Didn't want to give Wendy any reason to twist this night into something other than what it should be: Spencer's triumph. Her moment.

But he couldn't bring himself to walk away either.

So he hovered a few feet away, sipping one of the champagnes, trying to look casual. Trying not to look like a man who'd just had the wind knocked out of him by an emerald dress—and the powerhouse woman wearing it.

Chapter Three

Wendy Rakowski's timing was both perfect and terrible. She was the distraction Spencer needed to fend off the panic. Spencer smiled past the journalist, hoping he would know it was just for him.

She may have needed the distraction—but she didn't *want* it.

"Spencer! I've been dying to talk to you. The film was incredible, every bit as good as the book. Where did the story come from?"

She forced herself to smile, breathing through the thudding in her chest. "It's been... years in the making. Not the story itself, exactly, but the skills that brought it to life."

"Was it based on personal experience?"

The question made her throat tighten. She glanced, instinctively, over Wendy's shoulder—only to lock eyes with Jace.

He was still there.

Still watching her, smiling.

And somehow, she didn't panic.

She turned back to Wendy, her voice soft but steady. "There's a bit of reality in every piece of fiction. It's up to you to figure out just where they are."

Wendy nodded, jotting notes. "You've written other novels, right?"

"Yes," she said. "Four others. But for some reason, *Fighting Gravity* is the one that resonated with the world."

"Where did you learn to write like this? Your characters, your scenes... they have this *weight* to them."

That made her laugh—genuinely this time. "I had some amazing college professors, right here at Michigan State University. Read a lot of the classics. *Anne of Green Gables* taught me how to feel. *The Great Gatsby* taught me how to write pain with restraint."

What she didn't say? The truth behind the curtain.

That there were old notebooks under her bed and dusty floppy disks in a box marked "Taxes" that held hundreds of thousands of words she'd once shared on internet fan boards. Entire epic romances starring characters suspiciously resembling boy band members. Her earliest readers had been teenage girls with usernames like "ILuvJoeyJoe" and "JC4Ever98."

They had been her first audience. Her first cheerleaders.

She hadn't written for validation. She had written because it made her *feel*.

And now, the boy bander who unknowingly inspired half those stories was standing just a few feet away... with two glasses of champagne and something that looked dangerously close to reverence in his eyes.

Oh, how would she ever survive this night?

□□□

He caught her glance. The confident nod of her head. The way her spine straightened as she answered the questions with grace and humility. That soft smile that looked like it was meant just for him.

Or was that part his imagination?

She was the real deal.

Not just talented. Not just beautiful.

Resilient.

He waited until Wendy thanked her and stepped away. Then he moved forward, extending one of the glasses with a nervous chuckle.

"Hi," he said. "You're Spencer Callahan."

"I am," she said. His heart skipped as she smiled at him. "And you are Jace Rose. I'm a big fan."

"I'd like to say the same," he said. "But I, uh... I didn't read the book."

She blinked, lips quirking. "No?"

He shook his head, sheepish. "Not even the script. Had no idea what I was walking into tonight. I assumed it was going to be... light. Romantic fluff."

Her eyebrow arched. "And what led you to that conclusion?"

There was no judgment in the question, no accusation. Just curiosity.

"The song lyrics," Jace told her. "I read them, and thought since it was another generic love song, that this was probably a fluffy rom-com."

"Generic love song?" She smiled, but it was tight, and Jace was suddenly afraid he had offended her.

"Okay, so maybe generic is a bit harsh," he said quickly. "The lyrics needed a little polish. I tweaked them a bit before writing the music."

Her eyes sparkled, and the corner of her mouth lifted in a teasing curve. "That was you?" she asked, mock scandalized. "You're the one who changed my lyrics? They weren't good enough for the great Jace Rose to sing as written?"

He held up a hand, laughing softly. "I didn't say that. They weren't bad, exactly. In fact, they were good. Really good. They just needed a little...push. Something that fit this melody I couldn't shake. I hope you don't mind."

Spencer wanted to say that she did mind, just to tease him, just to see him flustered a little bit. She'd caught the look on his face when she questioned his use of the term "generic love song" and how back tracked to avoid upsetting her. It was cute. She wanted to see if she could frustrate him again, make that little bit of a blush creep up his neck and into his cheeks. But she found it impossible to do when her mind was screaming in all caps:

HE SAID THE LYRICS WERE GOOD. JACE ROSE, THE BOY WITH THE GOLDEN VOICE, WHO SANG THE SOUND TRACK OF MY TEENAGE YEARS, SAID MY SONG LYRICS, THE FIRST ONES I EVER WROTE, WERE GOOD. *REALLY GOOD.*

She managed to nod like a normal, functioning human being and not the crazed fangirl who used to doodle "Mrs. Jace Rose" in the margins of her Algebra notebook.

"Of course I don't mind," she said lightly. "It was the first time I even attempted song lyrics. I didn't expect them to be perfect."

Jace nearly choked on the champagne he'd just sipped. "Wait, what?" he said when the coughing subsided and he was able to speak. "You never wrote song lyrics before?"

Spencer gave a sheepish shake of her head. "I like to listen to music. But I never learned to play an instrument, though Mrs. Hammerslee did try to teach me violin in the fifth grade." Jace grinned at her. "I always assumed I'd need to know something about composing music to write a song. Plus," Spencer looked around, then leaned closer to Jace as if to share a deep secret, "I hate poetry. Never could decide if it was worse torture to study poems of others or to write my own. And song lyrics are too much like poetry."

Jace leaned in slightly, captivated now. "You *hate* poetry but wrote some of the most emotionally wrecking lyrics I've ever sung?"

She shrugged, the corner of her mouth curving with amusement. "Desperation's a hell of a motivator."

He laughed, low and warm. "So let me get this straight... You wrote your first-ever song lyrics on a whim, didn't think they were any good, and somehow still managed to write the only words that have haunted me for weeks?"

Spencer tilted her head. "Haunted you?"

Jace nodded, serious now. "There's a line in the second verse. *'I didn't lose myself, I gave myself away.'* That one stopped me cold the first time I read it. I had to walk around the studio for, like, ten minutes before I could sing anything."

Her breath caught. That line had come to her in the dark, long after she should've been asleep. She'd written it in the Notes app on her flip phone, terrified she'd forget it by morning.

"You kept that line," she said softly.

"Of course I did," he said. "It was perfect."

□□□

The look in his eyes was too much, too intense for her to process. Spencer needed to change the subject.

"If you didn't read the book," she asked, trying to keep her tone casual, "why did you agree to record the song? It can't be because my lyrics were so amazing."

"The ladies in my life talked me into it."

And there it was. Spencer felt the smile on her face falter, though she tried to hold it as long as she could. "Ladies?" she repeated, before draining the last of the champagne from her glass. The night had been going to well, had been too close to perfect. Of course, there was someone else in his life. A man could not look that good in a tux, sing like an angel, make her laugh so easily, and not have a special someone in his life.

Jace glanced over Spencer's shoulder, waved, then angled their bod-
ies so they were both looking across the garden. "My ladies," he said,
a note of pride in his voice, waving to a pair of women, standing
side-by-side near the edge of the garden. The older one smiled and
nodded as she sipped her red wine, the younger bounced on the balls
of her feet, looking as if she would jump right out of her heels any
moment from excitement. "My mother and sister. Heather is probably
your biggest fan. She's read all of your books, at least twice. When I told
her I'd been asked to be a part of the soundtrack..." He gave Spencer a
half-shrug, boyish and sheepish all at once. "I didn't want to do it. I've
had enough of singing in the spotlight. But she said she'd never speak
to me again if I didn't do it."

"And you actually want to speak to your sister?" Spencer teased.

Jace laughed. "Some days, she's not so bad."

"She's really read my books?" Spencer asked, trying to keep her
voice level. Even with the success of *Fighting Gravity*, it was still hard
to wrap her head around the idea that people wanted to read what
she's written, that complete strangers cared about the characters she
created. "All of them? Even *Broken By You*, which has got to be the
sappiest love story ever written?"

"More than once," he said. "Says the characters are real, and when
she puts one of your books away, it's like saying good-bye to a good
friend."

Spencer's hand fluttered to her throat. "Oh," she breathed. "That
has got to be the greatest compliment I've ever received. She's so sweet."

"And Mom," Jace continued, "she said *Fighting Gravity* changed
her. She cried throughout the entire thing. Sad tears, happy tears,
laughing tears. She said it was the most hopeful sad story she's ever
read."

Spencer didn't know whether to swoon, sob, or kick off her stilettos and run around the garden screaming, *Jace Rose's mom read my book and cried!!*

She managed a breathy laugh instead. "Well... I owe them both a thank-you." She smiled at Jace. "Would you mind introducing us?"

"Are you kidding?" He took the empty champagne flute from her hand and deposited it, along with his, on the empty tray of a server passing by. "I don't think they will let me get on the plane back home if I don't...and I bought their tickets."

He offered her his arm. As she placed her hand in the crook of his elbow, and he covered it with his strong, firm fingers, she felt her heart flip. Her grip tightened on the fabric of his jacket, holding her in place. She smiled wider. *You are Spencer Callahan, award-winning author. Grown. Ass. Woman. Act like it.*

But her heart refused to listen. That close to him, his fingers warm and steady on hers, she felt like the giddy teenager, ready to pass out because her crush smiled at her from the concert stage.

"Tell me," Spencer said as they made their way through the crowd, "should I be more nervous about meeting your mother or meeting my biggest fan?"

"Honestly? You should be terrified of Heather." Jace smiled and nodded at someone he recognized from the red carpet earlier, though he could not place the man's name. "She is going to either hug you or cry. Or both. And she was a wrestler in college. The girl has a grip like a grizzly bear. Plus, she is an ugly crier. She could capture you in an impossible vice grip while slobbering over you like a teething toddler. You have been warned."

Spencer laughed, nerves and giddy adrenaline tangling in her chest. "Good to know. Maybe I should've worn shoulder pads instead of a strapless gown."

Jace grinned. "Might've helped. But hey—if she takes you down, I'll pull her off. Eventually."

"Eventually?"

"Depends how entertaining it is."

She gave him a look, but there was no real heat behind it. Just amusement. And maybe a flicker of something else. Something brighter.

Jace patted her hand. "As for Mom, there's nothing to worry about there. She's a pushover."

"Yeah?"

"Yeah. She'll love you as long as I do."

They both froze.

Not fully—but just enough that the air changed. Jace blinked, as if realizing the words a split second too late. Spencer opened her mouth, then closed it, unsure if she should respond or pretend it hadn't happened.

Before either could say anything, a man with a festival badge stopped in front of them.

"Spencer Callahan?" he asked breathlessly. "Your panel last year—your thoughts on narrative honesty—I've never forgotten it. Thank you. Thank you for this story."

Spencer smiled automatically, grateful for the interruption and overwhelmed by it all at once. "That means so much," she said, her voice steady even as her hand gripped Jace's arm a little tighter.

They stepped away after a moment, but not three steps later, an older woman touched Spencer's arm. "You're the reason I started writing again," she said softly, eyes damp. "Thank you."

Spencer could only nod.

Jace didn't say a word through the next few moments. Just stayed close, hand steady on hers, eyes occasionally flicking to her face like he couldn't quite believe he was walking next to her.

They were nearly to the garden's edge when an older couple stepped into their path.

"Excuse me, An—" The woman stopped herself, eyes softening. "Spencer?"

Spencer blinked. Recognition dawned slowly, then all at once. "Mrs. Keller?"

The woman smiled, her hand already reaching for Spencer's. "It's so good to see you, sweetheart. We weren't sure you'd remember us."

"Of course I do," Spencer said, her voice catching slightly. Her hand slipped off of Jace's arm and she hugged the older woman, then shook hands with the man. "You lived across the street. You always bought lemonade, even when we forgot the sugar."

Mr. Keller gave a quiet nod. "We almost didn't come tonight. Big crowds, late nights... not really our thing anymore. But when we saw that you'd be here, we just... we had to."

Mrs. Keller still hadn't let go of her hand. "We haven't forgotten her, you know. Her smile. Her laugh. That spark of life that lit up the entire neighborhood, and how it was just... erased when they let that man into their home."

Spencer's breath hitched. The night was glitter and praise and surreal perfection. But this—this was what it was really about. That friendship. The innocence they lost. The girl who never got to grow up.

Mrs. Keller's eyes shimmered as she added, "The way you've honored her... it's just beautiful."

Spencer swallowed hard. She didn't trust her voice right away. She folded her arms gently across her middle, blinking back the burn behind her eyes.

"That's why I wrote it," she said softly. "So someone would remember her... like that."

"We're so proud of you," Mrs. Keller said. "And I know wherever she is tonight, she is, too."

They exchanged a few more soft words before the Kellers moved on, disappearing into the garden's soft lighting.

Jace said nothing at first. Just stood beside her, waiting for Spencer to collect herself, his body a shield from the cameras as she did so.

"You okay?" he asked gently.

"Yeah," Spencer said, her voice shaky. "I'm fine."

Jace looked at her and saw the tears shining in her eyes. "Spencer, are you lying to me?"

"Of course not." She blinked rapidly, forcing the tears away. Spencer placed her hand back on his arm and smiled up at him. "Jace, I never lie."

"Never?" He raised an eyebrow.

"Never," she repeated. "I just write fiction."

Chapter Four

♥

They continued across the garden together, moving slowly because everyone kept stopping her.

"Spencer, can we get a picture?"

"Oh, that ending! It tore at my heart, in the best way."

"Spencer, I just wanted to say congratulations."

"I have the book at home, but I just had to buy another copy. Would you sign it for me?"

Jace stayed close through every interruption, offering small smiles, occasionally glancing down at her like *she* was the headliner. And every time someone called her name or praised her work, he looked a little more...

Was that pride?

She felt it. That flutter in her chest. The disbelief that someone she used to watch perform at award shows now looked at *her* like she was the star.

"I thought tonight couldn't get any more surreal," she said quietly. "Then you started looking at me like that."

Jace smiled. "Like what?"

"Like I matter."

"You do matter."

"Really?" Her heart stuttered, threatening to leap right out of her chest. She leaned closer to him and whispered, "Then why are you introducing me to the grizzly bear?"

They reached the edge of the garden just as two women turned to face them—one elegant in a slate-blue dress, the other barefoot, holding her heels in one hand and visibly vibrating with excitement.

"Oh, it's her!!" the younger one whispered, loud enough for Spencer to hear.

Spencer barely had time to react before the younger woman let out a squeal and took off running, heels swinging, arms already open.

Jace grinned. "Brace for impact."

Spencer, fearing her stilettos wouldn't survive the incoming collision, ducked behind him. "Good advice," she whispered, peeking around his arm. "Don't fall on me, okay?"

Heather skidded to a stop and immediately threw her arms around Spencer, nearly lifting her off the ground.

"Oh my *gosh,* you're real! You're actually real!"

Spencer laughed, slightly breathless. "So I've been told."

"I've read *everything* you've ever written. *Twice.* I have a signed hardback of *Fighting Gravity* and a paperback of *Broken By You* that looks like it survived a hurricane. You made me cry on a plane, in a grocery store parking lot, and once during a staff meeting. Full-on ugly tears. The principal thought I was having a breakdown and wasn't sure I was fit to teach children. The English teacher demanded I start a book club."

"Okay, Heather." Jace pried his sister's arms from around Spencer and eased her back a step or two. "Remember your strength. We don't want to break the author."

"Sorry," Heather said, a slight blush creeping up her cheeks. "I'm just so excited to meet you. I've been a fan since my college roommate shared *Broken By You* with me. You write so beautifully."

Spencer laughed, a tendril of auburn hair escaping from one of her sparkling hairclips. As Jace watched it settle against her face, he found himself wondering if it felt as soft as it looked. And what did those auburn waves smell like? He was so lost in his thoughts that he barely registered the reply she made to his sister.

"You read *that* first and still wanted to keep going?" Spencer asked, raising a skeptical eyebrow. "Either you're not a student of literature, or your mother raised you with wonderful manners."

Heather grinned. "Maybe a little of both. But even if it was a Hollywood-worthy story, your characters were so...real. I swear, Miss Callahan, I like them better than most people." She smiled wider and bounced her head from side to side. "And I'm a people person."

A soft chuckle came from just behind them.

Spencer turned—and immediately straightened up.

The older woman stood with an elegance that didn't need effort. Her slate-blue dress caught the light just enough to hint at understated glamour, and the tilt of her head said she missed nothing. But her eyes... her eyes were warm.

Jace placed a hand at the small of Spencer's back and said softly, "Spencer, this is my mom. Carol Anne Rhodes."

Carol Anne extended her hand, not in some stiff, formal way—but like she meant it. Like she *saw* Spencer.

"It's a pleasure to finally meet you," she said. "Though I admit, it feels a bit like meeting someone I already know."

Spencer shook her hand, managing a small smile. "I feel like I should apologize in advance for all the awkward metaphors in *Summer Love.*"

Carol Anne's smile widened. "I'll only accept that apology if you promise to sign my copy later."

That earned a laugh from Spencer, who immediately felt some of the tension ease from her shoulders.

Heather, standing a half-step behind her mother, leaned in and whispered, "Told you she'd cry."

"I'm not crying," Carol Anne said primly. "Yet."

Spencer laughed again, the tension finally loosening in her chest. These people didn't just tolerate her—they *liked* her. And somehow, that was even more terrifying.

But before she could retreat behind another quip, Carol Anne's expression shifted—just slightly. Softer. Quieter.

"Can we talk about *Fighting Gravity*?" she asked. "I mean, I know you're probably sick to death of discussing it, but..." She let out a breath and touched the base of her throat, as if grounding herself. "It's just so beautiful."

Spencer blinked. "That's kind of you to say."

"I'm serious." Carol Anne looked her in the eye. "There's a line in it—page 242, I think. About how healing doesn't always look like strength. That sometimes, just choosing to keep breathing is the bravest thing a person can do."

Spencer went still.

Carol Anne smiled gently. "I've lived that. More than once. And reading it in your words... it felt like someone finally said it out loud."

Spencer swallowed hard, her voice barely above a whisper. "That line almost didn't make it into the final draft. I thought it was too raw. Too... mine. But my editor...well, she thought it needed to be there."

"Well," Carol Anne said, eyes misting over, "thank you for listening to her. I think it's something a lot of people needed to hear."

Carol Anne grinned and wiggled her eyebrows. "Even better than reading that line was seeing the scene on screen, and hearing that line delivered by someone as tasty as Jake Gyllenhaal..."

"Mother!"

She laughed at the horrified look on her son's face. "What? I know you don't like to admit it, son, but I am a fully functioning woman. I can still appreciate a good looking man." She took a dainty sip of her wine and added, "And that is one good looking man."

"Is this a good time to say hello?"

The voice came from just behind her, smooth and familiar. Without turning—and even without the deer-caught-in-the-headlights look on Carol Anne's face—Spencer knew who it was. Jake Gyllenhaal. Dressed in a sleek black suit, hands in his pockets, that effortless grin on his face.

"Oh my," Heather whispered under her breath.

The conversation froze like someone had hit pause. Jake stepped closer, his tone playful.

"I'm sorry, am I interrupting something? You all seemed to be having such a good time over here, but the second I showed up... silence. Should I go?"

"*NO!*" Carol Anne and Heather said in unison.

Beside her, Jace groaned. Spencer cleared her throat, praying her cheeks weren't on fire. "Jake, this is Carol Anne Rhodes—Jace's mom and a very, very gracious reader. And his sister, Heather."

Jake smiled. "Pleasure to meet you both."

He reached for Carol Anne's hand first, lifting it to press a soft kiss to the back. "And may I just say, that color is stunning on you."

Carol Anne looked like she'd briefly forgotten how to breathe. "The pleasure is all mine, Mr. Gyllenhaal."

Jake turned to Heather next and offered his hand with a wink. "Do I get to shake yours, or are you going to tackle me like you did the author?"

Heather blinked. "I—uh—handshake. Yes. We do handshakes."

He grinned. "Not that I'm against tackling, mind you. Just... not at a first meeting. And not in front of an audience."

Heather made a strangled noise and promptly offered him the wrong hand—the one still clutching her heels.

Jake glanced down at the strappy shoes hanging awkwardly in front of him and raised an eyebrow. "Thanks," he said smoothly, "but I don't think they're my size."

Heather let out something between a gasp and a squeak, yanked the shoes behind her back like she'd just flashed him by accident, and thrust her other hand toward him. "Right! Sorry! Normal handshake! Totally normal behavior here!"

Jace groaned into his palm. "I swear I'm not related to them."

Spencer was *dying*. Just when she thought she could hold in her laughter no longer, she noticed Nora, her agent, on the other side of the garden waving for her attention.

Before she could excuse herself, Jake leaned in slightly and murmured, "Looks like someone needs you. Don't worry—" he gave a quick glance at Carol Anne and Heather, both of whom were still hovering somewhere between euphoric and stunned—"I think I can entertain these two while you continue to charm your adoring public."

Spencer gave him a grateful smile. "You're a saint."

He winked. "No, I just play one on the big screen."

Jace snorted. "That tracks."

Spencer touched Carol Anne's arm gently. "I'll find you again before the end of the night, I promise."

Carol Anne nodded, but her eyes didn't leave Jake.

Heather waved vaguely, still clutching her shoes like a bouquet.

Jace took Spencer's hand and whispered, "Let's go. Before my mother proposes."

"If she does, are you gonna call Jake *Daddy*?"

Jace glowered at her but didn't answer.

Spencer chuckled as they walked away, her fingers twining naturally in his. "Tasty, huh?"

"Do not start," Jace warned.

She leaned in closer. "Fully functioning woman?"

"Spencer."

Chapter Five

♥

They drifted a few steps away while introductions carried on. Just as Jace opened his mouth to ask her something, another fan appeared.

"Spencer, can I take a picture with you? I swear I'll scream if I don't!"

Spencer laughed and posed, murmuring apologies to Jace.

Then another. A journalist. A blogger. A girl who said she ran an online book club on MySpace.

"You've really blown up," Jace said quietly, after the fifth interruption. No trace of annoyance—only quiet awe.

She looked up at him, surprised. "Sorry. This isn't... normal for me."

He shook his head, eyes still on her. "Don't be sorry. You earned this."

And there it was again.

That look.

Like he was proud of her. Like he'd known her longer than one evening. Like he'd seen something in her story that now lived in *her*.

She suddenly didn't want to be anywhere else.

"Besides, I have a feeling you'll need to adjust your definition of normal," Jace told her. "If this movie gets as big as I think it will, you're not going to get a moment of peace for the next few months."

She smiled up at him. "So I should take full advantage of any quiet time I get now?"

Spencer didn't even realize she'd stepped closer to Jace, not until he smiled, cupped her face with the softest touch she'd ever experienced, and whispered, "Exactly."

He tilted his head toward her. She stretched her neck, closed her eyes, and waited for the brush of his lips against hers.

Instead, she was jolted back to reality by a firm hand on her shoulder and the disapproving voice of her agent in her ear.

"Sorry, Spence," Nora said, wearing that tight-lipped *I'm saying the words but I'm 100% not sorry* smile that usually preceded deadlines, camera calls, or a mad dash through an airport terminal. "We've got a redeye to catch. Busy day tomorrow. *Today Show* at eight. *Live with Regis and Kelly* right after, then *The View* at eleven. New York waits for no one."

Spencer's heart sank. "Now?" She turned to Jace, reluctant. "Just a few more minutes?"

Nora sighed. "Ten. Max." She backed away, holding up both hands—fingers splayed—then pointed at her watch.

Spencer nodded, then turned fully toward him. "I should've known my Cinderella moment would end with a countdown."

Jace chuckled. "You're leaving tonight?"

She nodded. "NYC mornings come early. Apparently, America needs to see my face while they're drinking coffee."

"Can't blame them," he said. "It's almost as breathtaking as the sunrise."

She laughed softly. "Only because I have a team of makeup artists helping me. If you saw me right out of bed, you might think differently."

He raised an eyebrow, his smile slow. "Maybe someday we can find out."

"Will you be at the L.A. premiere in two weeks?" she asked, trying to sound casual.

Jace's lips quirked. "Will that be my chance to wake up with you?"

Her breath caught. Eyes wide. Words? Gone.

He laughed. "Sorry. That was... a bit much."

She opened her mouth, closed it, then finally managed a breathy, "A little."

"I've been invited," he said, tone gentler now. "Haven't decided if I'll go or not."

"Oh." Her voice dipped. "I was hoping..."

His gaze sharpened. "Hoping for what?"

Spencer hesitated, then looked up at him—vulnerable, just a touch embarrassed. "The song. Now that I know you rewrote my words, I'd like to hear you sing it. Not a recording. Just... you."

Something shifted in his expression. "We might be able to make that happen." A beat. "If I do come... could I be your escort for the evening?"

She blinked, surprised by the smoothness, the warmth, the offer itself. "You're serious?"

"Deadly."

She paused. Then: "Okay. Yes. But under one condition."

He raised a brow. "Anything."

"You have to read the book first."

Jace gave a mock-groan. "I *knew* there'd be homework."

"Consider it prep," she said. "I'm told it's helpful to know the source material."

He laughed again, that signature grin softening into something quieter. More sincere. He pulled his phone from his pocket.

"Phone number?" he asked.

They exchanged numbers—quick, casual, but with that unmistakable buzz of *this means something*.

And just before she turned to leave, swept away toward the elevators and jet-fueled obligations, she acted on impulse.

Standing on her toes in her heels, she leaned in and kissed his cheek—light, warm, and just barely there.

He didn't move. Didn't speak.

Just smiled—slow and real—like she'd given him the first line of a song he hadn't known he was meant to write.

"See you in LA?" he asked.

She glanced over her shoulder, already being pulled away. "Only if you've finished the book."

□□□

Jace watched as Spencer, led by a rapidly moving agent plowing her way through the crowd, made her way to the exit. She stopped, to the obvious annoyance of her agent, at the swag table. He saw her pick up a pen and a hardcover copy of *Fighting Gravity*. With a smile, she opened the cover and scribbled something quickly inside. She looked up, somehow knowing he was watching her. She placed the book at the bottom of the stack and gave him a subtle wink.

And then she was gone.

The phantom feel of her kiss on his cheek lingered like the final note of a song. He reached up, brushing the spot with his fingers.

He should have said more.

He should have kissed her back.

But she was heading to New York, and in a few hours, he would be Los Angeles bound. He had exactly one thing he could do to let her know he was thinking of her while an entire continent separated them.

Read. That. Book.

He scanned the garden until he spotted his mom and Heather chatting animatedly near the catering table, forks in hand, dessert plates mostly ignored.

He strode over, that distant, dazed smile still playing on his face.

"Are you two ready to go?"

Carol Anne blinked. "Now? But the party's not even winding down."

Heather narrowed her eyes at him. "Why are we leaving early? You love a good party."

Jace slipped his hands into his pockets, looking vaguely stunned and deeply certain all at once.

"Because I think I just met the girl I'm gonna spend the rest of my life with."

Heather's fork, the perfect bite of raspberry-topped cheesecake balanced precariously on top, froze halfway to her mouth.

Carol Anne clutched her chest and whispered, "Oh my stars. Jason, really?"

He didn't say anything. He just smiled, and that was answer enough.

Desserts forgotten, they followed Jace toward the exit. He paused at the small display of her books, bypassing the first five on the stack until he reached the one on the bottom. He ran his fingers over the cover she had so recently touched before opening the book.

Inside, on the front page, written in looping, careful script:

To the voice behind the music

May my words live in your heart the way your melodies live in mine.

—Spencer

His eyes lingered on the message. No last name. No fanfare. Just a note.

One he knew was meant only for him.

He closed the book gently.

"Let's go."

Chapter Six

♥

She'd barely made it past security before the first text from him lit up her phone. Three days later, they were still going—half banter, half book club, all dangerously addictive.

Jace: Los Angeles (Pacific Time – PT)

Spencer: Michigan (Eastern Time – ET)

Jace – 7:01 PM PT Hey, Scribe! You busy?

Spencer – 10:02 PM ET Ah, Rockstar! Never too busy for you.

Jace – 7:05 PM PT I have your book in hand. A comfy chair to curl up in. And a glass ready for wine.

Spencer – 10:05 PM ET It's been three days since the premiere. I was starting to think you changed your mind about escorting me to the premiere.

Jace – 7:06 PM PT Never. Been a busy week. Just one question before I start reading...

Spencer - 10:06 PM ET What's that?

Jace – 7:07 PM PT Red wine? Or white?

Spencer – 10:08 PM ET Red. Always red. Unless you're starting Chapter 8. Then you'll need something stronger.

Jace – 7:09 PM PT That sounds like a challenge. Did it take something stronger to write it?

Spencer - 10:10 PM ET I'm not telling you all of my writing secrets...Don't know you that well yet

Jace – 7:11 PM PT Should I stretch first? Hydrate?

Spencer – 10:12 PM ET You said just one question That's two...

Jace – 7:13 PM PT Never been good with math

Spencer - 10:14 PM Same. That's why I write. You've got the wine for hydration. Might wanna stretch if you throw books when fictional characters disappoint you.

Jace – 7:15 PM PT Did you name a character after an ex? Or someone you wanted to throat-punch in high school?

Spencer – 10:16 PM ET Legally? Pure coincidence. Emotionally? I might've been working through a few things.

Heather – 7:33 PM PT Did I leave my hoodie at your house? The gray UCLA one. If you wash it, don't put it in the dryer. If you shrink it, I'm gonna glitter bomb your car, J

Jace – 7:36 PM PT Leave me alone, Grizz. I'm busy.

Heather – 7:38 PM PT GRIZZ? Who the heck is that??

Heather – 7:39 PM PT WAIT. Are you texting someone? Like... a *girl* someone?? WHO IS SHE?? DO I KNOW HER?? Do I LIKE her?? Do I need to start threatening her with glitter too??

Jace – 7:41 PM PT Calm down, Sis. And if you insist on greeting everyone with bear hugs, you gotta accept being called Grizzly Bear. Grizz.

Heather – 7:41 PM PT Bear hugs? OMG! Jace! Are you texting her? Spencer Callhan???

Jace – 7:42 PM PT Goodnight, Heather.

Jace – 7:43 PM PT Damn. Didn't expect that. She pushed him off the dock?? He didn't deserve that!

Spencer – 10:44 PM ET So you've met Chapter 6. That was fast. Do you realize how many *weeks* it took me to write the chapters you just finished in under thirty minutes?

Jace – 7:45 PM PT So I should slow down? Savor the prose? Drink between chapters?

Spencer – 10:46 PM ET Sip the wine. Throw the book. Curse the author. Whatever feels right.

Jace – 7:47 PM PT Was that a typo? Did you mean *kiss* the author? Cuz that feels about right.

Spencer – 10:50 PM ET Not a typo. But now you've got me thinking...

Jace – 7:52 PM PT Thinking about what?

Spencer – 10:53 PM ET Don't you wish you knew...

Jace – 7:54 PM PT Girl, you have no idea.

Spencer – 10:55 PM ET Boy, take a cold shower and keep reading.

Jace – 7:56 PM PT You'd like that, wouldn't you? Knowing you got me to take my clothes off?

Nora – 10:57 PM ET Quick reminder: You've got a bookstore signing Saturday at noon. Falling Rock Café & Bookstore in Munising, Michigan. They want to add a Q&A

Spencer – 10:58 PM ET I'm good with that, as long as it doesn't last more than 45 mins

Nora – 11:00 PM ET They're asking if you'll sign soundtrack CDs too.

Spencer – 11:01 PM ET Only if Jace Rose is there.

Nora – 11:02 PM ET It's kinda late notice, but I can reach out to his people...

Spencer – 11:01 PM ET Don't you dare. Besides, I'm talking to him right now

Jace – 8:02 PM PT Did I lose you?

Spencer – 11:03 PM ET Why would you think that?

Jace – 8:04 PM PT Thought that last line might have scared you off...

Spencer – 11:05 PM ET Do you look that bad without clothes on?

Nora – 11:05 PM ET What could you be talking to him about this late at night?

Jace – 8:06 PM PT Brutal. And no—I look amazing.

Spencer – 11:06 PM ET Just keeping him emotionally supported through Chapter 6. Very professional.

Nora – 11:07 PM ET Don't mix business with pleasure. No matter how hot he looks in a tux. Most guys clean up well. Doesn't mean they're not a waste of your time.

Nora – 11:08 PM ET Seriously, Spence. Keep the romance between the pages of your books.

Spencer – 11:08 PM ET There is no romance. And don't call me Spence.

Spencer – 11:09 PM ET I'll just bet you do...

Jace – 8:10 PM PT Girl, you are making it impossible for me to read this book. Do you... not want to see me next week?

Spencer – 11:11 PM ET Hey, if I had to write it while distracted, you can read it while distracted.

Jace – 8:32 PM PT Hey... I have to ask. Is this real? Or did you imagine all of it?

Spencer – 11:33 PM ET Some is real. Too much of it is real

Jace – 8:34 PM PT So...I'm reading about your life?

Spencer – 11:35 PM ET Not mine. But I watched it unfold. Someone I loved. I couldn't stop it. But I couldn't let it go untold.

Jace – 8:36 PM PT You told it beautifully. That film... doesn't even come close to this.

Spencer – 11:37 PM ET Thank you. I just hope it helps someone. Someone...who is struggling with...life

Jace – 8:39 PM PT Spencer...I know it helped me. I hope that makes it worth it.

Spencer – 11:41 PM ET She'd like you. A lot. Meeting you almost makes it worth it.

Jace – 9:01 PM PT You really wrote a sex scene with a library metaphor. I'm both deeply turned on and ashamed of my high school GPA.

Spencer – 12:01 AM ET My mom always said knowledge is sexy. You're welcome.

Spencer – 12:08 AM ET I'm sorry. I'd love to hear what you think of the rest, but I'm falling asleep.

Jace – 9:09 PM PT OK. Sweet dreams, Scribe

THE NEXT MORNING

Jace – 5:42 AM PT Spencer, that was the most beautiful story I've ever read. I'm glad she got her happy ending.

Jace – 5:44 AM PT And I think you deserve a hug for living through the not-so-happy one.

Jace – 5:46 AM PT See you in LA next week?

Spencer – 8:49 AM ET Seven more days. Looking forward to it.

Chapter Seven

♥

Spencer adjusted the strap of her carry-on as she rode the escalator down into the terminal. Her body was tired from the long flight, but her mind buzzed with the familiar mix of nerves and excitement. At the bottom, she scanned the crowd for the driver Nora promised would be waiting—placard in hand, her pseudonym printed in big block letters. Spencer Callahan. Just seeing it in print still gave her a thrill.

She was halfway through the arrivals area when she saw them.

Hydrangeas.

A huge bouquet in soft blue, periwinkle, and violet, held in the arms of someone entirely too familiar.

Her steps faltered.

Jace.

She blinked.

Had her mind blurred the lines between dreams and reality? After all those late-night texts, all those conversations that lingered long after she set the phone down—was he really here?

How could he possibly know?

Yet there he stood, holding the largest bouquet of hydrangeas she'd ever seen. Jace Rose. In a fitted charcoal jacket, white tee, jeans, and that smile. That ridiculous, heart-melting smile.

And in his hands—her favorite flowers. The ones she'd tucked into quiet corners of all five novels. The ones no one, not even Nora, had ever mentioned.

But he had noticed.

Behind her, Nora came to a slow stop. "Well, I'll be damned," she muttered. "He actually showed."

Then, tossing her blonde curls over one shoulder, she veered toward baggage claim with a final, half-teasing grumble. "Don't vanish on me, Spence. And if you do decide to stay elsewhere tonight, I'd appreciate a heads-up before I call the cops."

Spencer almost walked right past him, too stunned to trust what her eyes were telling her. The shock hit so hard she didn't even flinch at the nickname, didn't correct Nora, didn't roll her eyes. Just stopped in her tracks and stared, blinking like an idiot.

"I didn't think I'd see you until Sunday," she said softly.

"That was the plan." His smile turned sheepish. "But then I thought... you've never been here. And I couldn't let you spend your first night in LA with room service and hotel art."

"But I didn't tell you my airline. Or the flight. Or when I'd land. How did you—?"

"Your agent," he said simply. "I had my manager call and get the information. I figured you might like to see a friendly face when you stepped out of the terminal."

She opened her mouth, then closed it again. A tentative hand reached out to touch his arm. He was real. He was warm.

"You're really here?"

"I am," he confirmed, smiling as he held out the flowers. "And these are for you."

She took them with trembling hands. "Hydrangeas? How did you know?"

"I read the book," he said, with a slight shrug of those broad shoulders. "Then I read the other four. You mention them in all of them. I figured... they had to mean something."

Her breath caught.

"They do." She inhaled their sweet scent. "Maybe I'll tell you about it sometime."

He tilted his head. "So... can I steal your Friday night? Dinner? A little sightseeing? I promise, no tourist traps. Let me show you my LA."

She gave a slow, stunned nod. "Okay."

A pause.

"And Jace?"

"Yeah?"

"I'm really glad your face was the first one I saw. Friendly or not."

He held out a hand. Her fingers curled into his, both their hearts racing as she took it.

□□□

Jace kept one hand on the wheel as they wove through the hills, the windows cracked just enough to let in the scent of eucalyptus and distant ocean. Spencer pulled his hoodie tighter around her, the sleeves still warm from when he'd handed it over at the airport.

"You good?" he asked, glancing sideways.

"Yeah," she said softly. "Just... taking it in. And wondering if you're warm enough without your hoodie. I didn't know LA nights could be so chilly."

He laughed, low and easy. "I'm fine. You forget—I survived that icebox of a premiere in East Lansing. After that, this feels like summer."

She smiled. "That theater was freezing," she shot back. "And my dress was strapless."

He gave her a sidelong glance. "Believe me, I noticed."

She snorted. "I'm not sure if I should be flattered or scared."

"Go with flattered," he said easily. "The scary part comes later."

She turned toward him, one eyebrow raised. "Why do I have a feeling that the scariest thing about you is your bear-wrestling sister?"

Jace laughed, low and warm. "You're not wrong. Heather once broke a guy's nose in college wrestling. And that was during practice."

"So I should probably stay on her good side?"

He glanced over again, softer now. "No problems there. You could break my heart seven ways to eternity, and she'd still love you. Me? If I so much as let you get a papercut, she'll make me pay for it for the rest of my life."

The silence stretched between them, soft and easy, like the lights outside the window—steady and glowing, never too bright.

The city sparkled below, all twinkle and sprawl, stretching as far as she could see. There was a low hum in her ears. Maybe a little bit adrenaline.

Maybe a little bit him. Maybe a lot him.

At a curve near the top, he slowed and pulled into a narrow turnout. The headlights cut across a rusted railing and the dark, open space beyond.

Jace shifted into park and leaned forward slightly, resting his arms on the steering wheel.

"I live up there," he said, nodding toward the silhouettes of houses scattered higher along the ridgeline. "But it felt a little soon to bring you home on a first date."

Spencer turned to look at him, lips parting. "Is that what this is? A date?"

He glanced at her then, a smile tugging gently at the corner of his mouth. "Unless you're planning to invoice me for your time."

She bit back a grin. "Just clarifying the terms. So I know what to tell Heather if I get a papercut."

He laughed, low and real, and the sound of it settled somewhere deep in her chest.

They didn't stay long—just a few minutes of quiet, the two of them watching the city breathe below them. Then he reached for the ignition again.

"Come on," he said. "I made us a reservation."

Chapter Eight

♥

The restaurant wasn't trendy or paparazzi-packed. It was tucked between a laundromat and a bookstore with faded awnings and string lights in the windows. Inside, the air was warm and smelled like rosemary and roasted tomatoes.

"Jace," the hostess said with a smile, "table for two?"

He nodded.

"You finally brought someone who's not your manager," she added with a teasing glance at Spencer before grabbing two menus. "About time."

Spencer glanced over, brow raised.

His arm around her waist, Jace leaned in slightly. "My manager's obsessed with their gnocchi. I've been here six times in the last month, and never once with someone I wanted to impress."

Her cheeks flushed as she looked away, smiling. "Well, now I feel pressure to like the gnocchi."

The hostess led them to a corner table near the window, then disappeared without another word. Jace pulled out her chair before taking the seat across from her.

"You don't have to like the gnocchi," he said softly, his eyes holding hers. "As long as you like the company."

"Jace, you don't have to try to impress me." Spencer smiled and reached across the table, placing a hand over his. "You could have given me peanut butter and jelly, and I still would have enjoyed your company."

"Really?"

She winked. "Sure, as long as you cut the crusts off."

His laugh came easy, genuine. "Noted. No crusts, extra charm."

"No extra charm," Spencer told him. "Just be you. That's impressive enough."

They talked. About the food. About the way the city looked from the hills. About *Fighting Gravity*—both the film and the book.

He admitted he'd cried during Chapter Seventeen.

She hesitated, then nodded. "That was the hardest scene I've ever written."

He watched her, quiet.

"I don't know if it was harder to write it for the book or the screenplay," she said, reaching for her ice water. "I wasn't on set that day. It was the one day I just couldn't be. Putting Cassie through it on paper was one thing. But Amy Adams is such an amazing actress. Watching her play that flashback, with the drugs, the abuse, the self-loathing... I knew I couldn't handle it."

Jace turned his wine glass slowly between his hands. "Was it really not about you?"

"No," Spencer said, with a slow, sad smile. "It really wasn't about me. It's a story I watched happen and was helpless to change. And it didn't have a happy ending. I guess writing it like I did, with Cassie and Max so happy together, that was my way of giving my friend the ending she deserved."

He looked up. "I think that's the most beautiful reason to tell a story."

□□□

Later, after the plates had been cleared and she'd stolen the last bite of tiramisu from his fork, he asked if she was too tired for one more stop.

"I *am* tired," Spencer admitted, "but I don't want this night to end. And I do want to see more of your world."

The drive west was quiet. The air had dropped another ten degrees, and the wind carried the scent of salt and pine. When he parked again, the city was gone—replaced by the hush of the ocean, vast and dark.

She climbed out slowly, eyes wide as the sound hit her first—rhythmic, constant, wild—and then the sight.

"It's so big," she breathed.

He grinned. "First time someone's said that to me and meant the ocean."

She gave him a look, but her smile lingered. "I mean it. I've never seen anything like this."

He reached for her hand. "Come on. It gets better the closer you get."

They walked the beach slowly, shoes dangling from their fingers, waves curling in and out like breath. Her toes were cold. Her nose was pink. But his hoodie was warm, and his presence even warmer. And his fingers, laced with hers, never let go.

"I needed this," she said softly. "This whole night. The quiet. The conversation." She looked away, then glanced back at him through her lashes. "Time with you."

He stopped walking. Turned to face her. Even in the moonlight, he was the most handsome man she'd ever seen.

She held his gaze, her heart thudding, certain he was going to kiss her.

But then a gust of wind hit, and her body betrayed her—shoulders shivering, teeth chattering.

He let out a soft laugh. "Okay, Snowflake. Let's get you to your hotel."

Before she could argue, he tugged her close, wrapping her in his arms as they turned back toward the car.

"This isn't over," he murmured near her ear. "But I'd rather your lips not be frozen when I finally kiss you."

She tilted her head, eyes dancing. "Aw. Is that what this is? You're feeling a little... inadequate next to the Pacific?"

He pressed a hand to his chest, mock wounded. "Brutal."

"The truth usually is."

He laughed, tightened his arm around her and kept walking.

And while she was disappointed that he hadn't kissed her, Spencer was willing to wait.

After all, this wasn't one of her romance novels or a fairytale. It was real life.

And the good things?

They were worth waiting for.

Chapter Nine

♥

They reached her hotel room slower than necessary, lingering in the quiet hall just outside the door. Jace stood close, his hands loose at his sides now, like he was giving her space but ready to close it if she asked. Spencer clutched the hydrangeas a little tighter, not because they were slipping—but because letting go might mean reaching for him instead. His hoodie still clung to her like a second skin, warm with memory.

She wondered what it would feel like if his arms could warm her the way his sweatshirt did.

"This was…" she started, then shook her head with a soft laugh. "Honestly? Kind of perfect."

He smiled. "Good. I was aiming for that. Wouldn't want total perfection on the first date, or I might disappoint you on the second."

She smiled, her green eyes sparkling. "I'm not sure you could ever disappoint me."

There was a pause. A soft one. The kind that held possibility.

"How long are you in LA?" he asked, voice low.

"I was planning to leave Tuesday morning, after the premiere," she said. "But honestly? I've got nowhere I need to be except at my keyboard." Her eyes lifted to his. "So... I could be persuaded to stay a bit longer."

His smile widened. "I'm pretty good at being persuasive."

She arched a brow. "Oh, I'll just bet you are."

He stepped closer—just slightly—but it was enough. Enough for her breath to catch, for her pulse to skip. The hallway was quiet. His gaze dipped to her mouth, then back to her eyes.

And just as he leaned in—

The door behind her swung open.

Nora stood there, fully dressed, holding a half-eaten protein bar and a hotel notepad.

"Don't mind me," she said flatly, stepping aside. "Just trying to finalize a press schedule while my client makes out in the hallway."

Spencer flushed. "Nora!"

Jace let out a low laugh and stepped back. "Guess that's my cue."

"Glad you can take a hint." Nora didn't bother closing the door—just slid back into the room, still chewing, flipping the page on her notepad as she walked.

Spencer gave him a look—half apology, half longing. "I'm sorry. She's... very committed to her job."

He shook his head. "It's okay."

Then he leaned in and kissed her just below her temple, where her skin was soft and cool from the night air. She closed her eyes at the warmth of it.

"Goodnight, Spencer."

She watched him walk down the hallway, heart pounding, hoodie sleeves pulled tight around her fingers. Only when the elevator doors closed behind him did she let out a breath.

Inside, Nora was already flipping through her notes like nothing had happened.

"One night, and you're already wearing his hoodie?" she said, not looking up. "This is real life, Spencer. Not one of your romance novels. Don't get caught up in a fairytale that's bound to fade."

Spencer didn't answer. She didn't even look Nora's way.

Some moments didn't need defending.

Not to someone who'd forgotten how to believe in them.

She set the flowers gently on the dresser and reached for her phone.

A soft smile tugged at her lips as she began to type.

□□□

He hadn't even reached the lobby when the first message came through.

Spencer – 11:58 PM PT Sorry about Nora. She tends to be an overprotective chaperone sometimes.

Jace smiled. He knew a little something about overprotective agents and managers acting as chaperones. Only he'd experienced it in his teens and early twenties. He felt for her, dealing with it at nearly thirty. He tapped out a message back, then hurried to the parking lot, already eager for her answer.

Jace – 12:00 AM PT If she hadn't opened the door...Would you have let me kiss you?

He reached his car while waiting for her answer. He sat in the driver's seat, drumming his fingers against the steering wheel as he waited.

Spencer – 12:05 AM PT If I had asked...Would you have taken me to see where you live?

Jace leaned back in his seat. He almost forgot how to breathe. It had been a long time since he'd taken a girl to his home. So long that he'd never brought one to this particular home, a house he'd built and moved into three years before. But the thought of having Spencer there with him... Even if all they did was sit together, talking long into the night, it would be the perfect ending to the perfect day.

Jace – 12:07 AM PT If I come back to your room now...Will you let me take you to my place?

Spencer – 12:08 AM PT Sorry. My jailer's never gonna let me leave now.

Spencer - 12:10 AM PT Sweet dreams, Jace.

Jace - 12:11 AM PT Only if they are of you.

Chapter Ten

♥

On Monday evening, the knock came precisely at 5:45, just like Nora had said it would.

Spencer smoothed the front of her gown one last time, her palms gliding nervously over the soft shimmer of champagne silk. The strapless bodice hugged her frame with quiet elegance, the fabric catching the light like candle glow. It didn't quite reach the floor, by design, her stylist had said, meant to show off the vintage-inspired heels and the pearl-dusted gloves that skimmed past her wrists. A single strand of pearls rested against her collarbone, understated and timeless, echoing the old Hollywood grace they had aimed for. Her hair was swept up, pinned in loose waves with delicate gold clips her stylist had called quietly romantic. Dangling pearl and gold earrings caught the light with every subtle movement, highlighting the warm sheen of her auburn hair.

She exhaled once, then opened the door.

And there he was.

Jace stood just outside, impossibly handsome in a black tuxedo worn without apology. Open collar, no tie. Classic and rebellious all at once. Of course he had shown up looking like a slow ballad come to life.

In one hand, he held a small bouquet of hydrangeas, pale blush, and soft violet, fresh and full. His expression held the kind of look that made her forget every line of dialogue she had ever written. Admiration. Wonder. Something tender and searching.

His gaze swept over her slowly, reverently. Not possessive. Not hungry. Just awestruck.

"You look," he said, voice low and husky, "like you stepped out of the pages of your book."

A flush rose to her cheeks. "I don't imagine I look that good."

He stepped forward, lifting the flowers. "No," he said softly. "You look better."

She opened her mouth, maybe to make some deflecting joke, maybe to thank him, but the words didn't come. Only the scent of hydrangeas and the steady rhythm of her heart, louder now, as he closed the final inch between them.

"Has no one ever told you how exquisitely beautiful you are?"

Exquisite? No, Spencer was sure that word had never been used to describe her appearance before. Her writing, maybe. The emotion in it, even the characters she created. But Spencer Callahan? Exquisite? She was sure she would remember that.

"No," she whispered. "At least not often enough for me to believe it."

He leaned toward her and pressed a tender kiss just below her cheekbone. Spencer's eyes closed, lost in the feeling of his lips lingering against her skin.

"I might have to do something about that," he murmured, his breath dancing lightly across her skin.

She hoped he meant it.

Jace pulled back slightly and held out the bouquet. She took it in trembling hands.

"But for now," he said, "we should go. There's a car waiting. And if I stare at you much longer, if I let my lips touch your skin again, I might never want to leave this room."

Spencer brought the flowers to her face, inhaling deeply, trying to calm the racing of her heart.

"That sounds like the making of a great Hollywood mystery," she said. She set the bouquet aside and exchanged it for a small clamshell clutch that matched her gown. "If I don't show up at this premiere, Nora is going to hunt you down and kill you." She smiled. "Though you would make one sexy corpse."

Jace grinned. "Sexy corpse? Spencer, you scare me."

She took the arm he offered, her laughter echoing off the hotel hallway as they stepped out of her room and the door closed behind them.

"Good," she said. "Just don't get on my bad side and you'll be fine."

□□□

The limo was quiet, a gentle hum beneath them as they inched through LA traffic. Outside, the glow of flashing lights painted streaks across the windows. Inside, the soft leather seats and dim lighting gave the illusion of calm.

Jace glanced at her.

Even in the shadows, he could see it. Her face had gone pale.

Her fingers, which had been resting loosely in her lap, now gripped her clutch like a lifeline. Her breaths came faster now, shallow, and uneven, like her body had forgotten how to pull in air properly. This wasn't just nerves. This was fear, tight and quiet and creeping up from the inside.

"Spencer?"

His voice was soft, barely more than a breath, but it found her anyway.

Her voice was rough, barely holding shape. "All those people…"

The next words came too fast, clipped, and uneven, like her brain was sprinting and her mouth couldn't keep up.

"So many more than East Lansing. What if I trip? What if the dress rips or my hair falls or my voice—" Her breath hitched. "What if I can't—"

He reached for her hand, lacing his fingers gently through hers.

"What if," he said softly, "you charm them all… the way you've charmed me?"

She jerked her hand back like it burned. Pressed her knuckles to her mouth. Tried to breathe.

"I'm serious, Jace. So much…could go…wrong."

He didn't laugh. Didn't tease. Just watched her, steady and present.

"There are just as many things that could go right," he said. "More, even."

She turned to the window, shoulders tight, chest rising too fast as the city lights grew closer.

"And even if something does go wrong," he said gently, "I'll be right beside you. Every step."

This time, when he reached for her hand, it was slow. Intentional. Steady. Solid.

She let him take it.

"Hold my hand if you want. Lean on me. You're not alone here, Spencer. I've got you."

Her eyes met his. Shaky, vulnerable, but softening.

"You've really got me?" she asked, needing to hear it one more time.

He gave her fingers a gentle squeeze. "Yeah," he said. "I do."

The car eased to a stop. There were still at least two cars ahead of them in line.

"Feel that?" he said, raising her hand and placing it against his chest. "That's me. My heart. Beating for you. Slow, steady. Try to breathe in time to that."

Her fingers trembled under his, but she nodded.

"You don't have to match it perfectly," he said. "Just try. In through your nose. Out through your mouth."

She did. Once. Then again. Still shaky. Still shallow. But slower now.

He kept his voice low, almost like a lullaby. "In... two, three... out... two, three..."

She closed her eyes and followed. Again. And again.

The lights outside flashed like camera bulbs, but in the hush of the car, it felt a world away.

Her shoulders dropped a little.

Her jaw unclenched.

The tightness in her chest started to give, just enough to breathe.

"Better?" he asked.

Her eyes opened, glassy but clear.

"Yeah," she whispered. "Better."

The driver glanced back through the mirror. "One more ahead of you, sir."

Jace nodded, never taking his eyes off her.

"You ready?"

She gave his hand a squeeze. "I will be. Just... don't let go."

"Never."

The car inched forward.

And this time, Spencer didn't flinch.

"Can we do this?" he asked.

She nodded. "I think so."

The door opened.

"Jace?" Spencer said, squeezing his hand. "Thank you."

He raised her hand to his lips and kissed her fingers. "Thank you for trusting me," he said.

□□□

Jace stepped out first, the flash of cameras immediate and blinding. He paused, calm and composed, offering a wave to the crowd like it was second nature. Like he belonged.

Then he turned, reaching back into the car.

Spencer took his hand.

Her heels hit the carpet. Her breath hitched. But Jace's fingers were warm around hers—steady, grounding. He didn't let go as he helped her to her feet, guiding her into the electric swirl of the LA evening air.

The noise swelled. The cheering turned thunderous, the flashes more insistent—because now they *saw* her. And it didn't take long for recognition to catch up with speculation.

The girl Jace Rose was escorting wasn't a starlet or another singer.

It was Spencer Callahan.

"Is this a new romance?" someone called out.

"How long have you two been together?" shouted another.

"Is this your *official* red carpet debut as a couple?"

Spencer paused, just for a moment. Long enough for her smile to begin to feel natural.

Jace stayed quiet. This was her night, her premiere, her moment. And he was proud—*so* damn proud—to stand beside her. He wanted to shout it, honestly. That he was hers. That he hoped like hell she might be his. That whatever this was, it felt too real to pretend otherwise.

But he let her take the lead.

And she shined.

With grace and confidence, Spencer answered the questions she wanted—about the film, about the adaptation process, about the way the cast brought her story to life. The personal ones? She redirected with ease. Laughed off the rest.

At one point, she glanced at him over her shoulder and said playfully, "I guess if readers want the inside scoop, they'll have to wait for my next book."

The press laughed. The cameras clicked. Jace couldn't take his eyes off her.

As they moved together down the carpet, he kept close—his hand resting on the small of her back, fingers linking with hers when she reached for him. Every few steps, they were asked to stop for photos. He never moved far. One arm around her waist. A subtle tilt toward her. A whisper, just for her, in between flashes.

Later, inside the theater, he stayed the same. Protective. Present.

His arm curled around her shoulders as the lights dimmed and her name appeared onscreen.

And in the dark, he whispered the only thing that felt big enough to hold it all:

"You were born for this."

"No, I was born to write," she whispered. "The rest of it? I'm just making up as I go along."

Chapter Eleven

♥

The Hollywood Roosevelt Hotel was bathed in soft gold and champagne light, every Art Deco detail glowing like it had been polished for the occasion. The pool shimmered just beyond the patio doors, but most of the guests lingered in the historic Blossom Ballroom, where velvet drapes and crystal sconces made even industry veterans pause to soak it in.

And just off the ballroom stage, the Brandon Juliet Quartet played a slow, dusky number—jazz with a heartbeat. The perfect soundtrack for everything Spencer couldn't yet put into words.

She stood just past the edge of the crowd, clutching a flute of prosecco she hadn't touched. Around her, congratulations drifted like confetti—"brilliant adaptation," "flawless dialogue," "that final scene wrecked me." A few dared to go further: "Award-worthy," "If this doesn't win an Oscar, my faith in this industry is dead." Spencer smiled, nodded, thanked them—but didn't let any of it sink too deep. Praise like that felt dangerous. Unsteady. Easier to laugh off than believe.

Jace was talking to someone from the soundtrack team, laughing, nodding—but his eyes kept drifting back to her. Like they had all night. Like he'd been doing since the moment she'd opened that hotel room door and saw him standing there in a tux with no tie and that damn smile.

He finally broke away from the group and walked toward her. He paused, a concerned look flittering across his face. Spencer watched as he slipped his phone from his pocket, flipped it open, and shook his head. The smile was firmly back on his face when he reached her side.

A muted buzz came from his pocket. Jace ignored it, focusing instead on Spencer.

"You survived the premiere," he said, voice low and warm.

"I did," Spencer said. "Wasn't sure there for a moment, after the red carpet. Some of those questions."

Another buzz from his pocket. Still, he didn't take his eyes off of the author. He chuckled. "You were amazing. Not giving them anything when they asked you about your personal life? Seasoned red carpet pros have a hard time deflecting the way you did."

Spencer lifted one shoulder. "How could I tell them the status of a relationship that I am unsure of?"

Jace stepped closer to her, closer enough that the pocket of his tux jacket brushed against her arm. Close enough that Spencer felt the vibration of his phone when it buzzed again.

"Do you need to check that?" she asked him. "It sounds like someone really wants to get a hold of you."

"It's just my sister." He waved his hand. "It's nothing."

"Are you sure?" she asked. "It could be an emergency. She's rather insistent."

"I'm sure," Jace said. "It's nothing to worry about."

They were silent for a moment, and the phone buzzed once again. Spencer looked at him and asked, "Jace, please will you check that? If something has happened to your mother or sister..."

"Nothing has happened to them," he assured her. "Yet." The concerned look in her eyes touched his heart. Jace realized in that moment that there were three women he would do anything for--his mother, his sister, and his new favorite author. He took the phone from his pocket, flipped it open, and handed it to Spencer. "See for yourself. Heather is perfectly fine."

Spencer took the phone, looked down, and saw a series of text messages from Heather to her brother. She read them out loud, laughing as she did.

Heather - 8:30 PM PT You said you were going to the premiere. You didn't say you were going as her date!!

She looked up at Jace. "You risked the wrath of the grizzly bear by not telling her that this is a date?"

"You didn't admit it to Wendy from *People*," he said. "No judgments."

She looked back at the phone.

Heather - 9:02 PM PT Jason David Rhodes, why didn't you tell me this was a DATE?

And the next message:

Heather - 9:07 PM PT Did you kiss her yet??

"Oh, she did not ask that," Jace said, reading the phone over Spencer's shoulder. "As if the first kiss is not awkward enough. Yeah, there's nothing wrong with Heather now, but wait until I get my hands on her..."

Then the final message, which Spencer could barely read through her laughter:

Heather - 9:15 PM PT ANSWER ME ALREADY! I'm dying here.

"Dying, yeah," Jace said, reaching for the phone. "She's dying all right."

Instead of handing the phone back to him, Spencer passed him her glass of prosecco. "Hold this," she said, her fingers flying over the keys of Jace's phone.

"Wait, what are you doing?" he asked her. "You're answering her? Spencer, what are you saying to her?"

She grinned up at him, then cast her eyes back to the phone. "Trust me."

"I'm not sure if I should."

With a flourish, Spencer hit the send button. "There," she said, handing the phone over and taking her drink back. "That should keep her happy." She sipped from her flute, watching as Jace read the message she'd sent.

Jace's eyes grew wide as he read:

Jace - 9:16 PM PT Hi, it's Spencer. He hasn't kissed me--yet. Maybe if you stop bugging him, he will have a chance to. --SC

"You did not..."

Spencer grinned at him over the rim of her glass. "So what if I did?" She looked as if she wanted to say more, but was interrupted by a journalist, wanting a quote for her morning article. For the next half an hour, they wandered through the room, Jace never leaving Spencer's side, as she answered questions, posed for pictures, and even signed a few copies of *Fighting Gravity*.

Jace's phone was silent the entire time.

When she needed a break, Spencer took hold of Jace's arm and tugged him into a quiet, dark corner. His eyes were wide with wonder as she stepped closer to him.

"You know," she said softly, "you could do it."

"Do what?"

"Kiss me."

His breath caught in his chest. "What did you say?"

She stepped even closer and reached her hand up to caress his cheek. "Kiss me, Jace."

He didn't move. Not at first.

So she let her fingers trail from his cheek, slow and certain, curling around the back of his neck. Her touch was light, but the message was clear.

She drew him just a little closer.

That's when he moved.

He leaned in, steady, sure. Because the only thing better than being kissed by Spencer Callahan... was kissing her first.

And when their lips met, it was the kind of kiss that silenced everything else. The jazz. The clinking glasses. The distant cameras. All of it fell away. There was only this.

She sighed against his mouth, fingers tightening at the nape of his neck. He responded with a low hum, his hand finding the small of her back, steadying her, holding her like something rare.

When they finally pulled apart, Jace didn't say anything at first. He just looked at her, wonder softening every line of his face.

Then, quietly, "Wow."

Spencer tilted her head. "What was that you said about the first kiss always being awkward?"

He smiled, brushing a loose strand of hair from her face, his fingers lingering near her temple.

"Yeah," he said. "It's supposed to be. We must've done something wrong."

She smiled back. "Perhaps we should try again."

He didn't need to be asked twice.

This time, he closed the space between them, one hand still at the small of her back, the other finding her jaw. He kissed her like a man who'd been waiting a long time to get something right. And Spencer met him there, with no doubt, no hesitation.

They didn't hear her approach.

"You two done playing leading roles in a romance novel?" Nora's voice came from just behind them, dry and amused and not far from mocking. "No sneaking off, lovebirds. The studio wants pictures with the author and the cast."

Spencer pulled back, cheeks flushed, but she didn't look embarrassed—just breathless. She rested her forehead against Jace's for a heartbeat before turning to Nora. "Do I have time to catch my breath?"

"Nope," Nora said, already steering her toward the ballroom. "You've got a film to sell."

As Spencer walked ahead, Jace made to follow—but Nora blocked his path with one perfectly manicured hand on his chest.

"I don't believe in love," she said, her tone cool and unshakable. "Not the way Spencer does. I don't believe in forever, or soulmates, or the idea that any of this—whatever this is—will last past the last camera flash."

Jace said nothing, eyes locked on Spencer across the room.

"But I do believe in Spencer. And I know she's carried more heartache than most people survive. So if you, Mr. Has-Been Boy Band Heartthrob, add to it, I swear to you, there will not be a corner of hell that will save you from me."

She let her hand drop and took a step back.

"And I'll smile while I destroy you."

Then she turned, walking away with all the grace and sharp edges of someone who never bluffed.

Jace didn't move right away.

He watched Nora disappear into the crowd, her words still ringing in his head. Not a threat. A promise.

And honestly? He didn't blame her.

Because if he were in her shoes—if he knew someone like Spencer, loved her, protected her—he'd feel the exact same way.

And the truth was, he already did.

Chapter Twelve

♥

His gaze drifted back to the ballroom.

Spencer was standing near the edge of the crowd, deep in conversation with Zach Braff and Amy Adams. Jake Gyllenhaal said something that made her laugh, and she reached up instinctively to tuck a loose strand of hair behind her ear. The gesture was small, but it hit Jace right in the chest.

She looked radiant. Grounded. A little overwhelmed, maybe, but she was holding her own. And somehow, in the middle of all of it, she still looked like *his* Spencer.

He crossed the room.

When she saw him, her smile shifted—brighter, warmer—but her brow knit just slightly. When he reached her, she leaned in and asked under her breath, "Everything okay?"

"Yeah," he said. "Why?"

She nodded subtly toward where Nora had stopped him. "She didn't say anything out of line, did she?"

Jace's mouth twitched. "She was perfectly respectable."

Spencer raised an eyebrow. "Nora? Respectable? Are you sure about that?"

He smiled, and for a second, he didn't say anything. Just looked at her like she was the only thing in the room that mattered.

Then, softly, "I'm sure about one thing tonight. And she's standing right in front of me."

Spencer froze. Just for a second. Just long enough for her heart to forget how to beat. And then—

"Come on," he said softly, reaching for her hand. "Let me dance with the woman who stepped out of my dreams... before I wake up and she's with someone better."

Spencer didn't smile at first. She just looked at him, eyes steady. "I've never met a better man, Jace. Not even in my dreams."

She let him lead her onto the small dance floor near the stage, where the Brandon Juliet Quartet was starting something new—soft, slow, and full of longing. The opening notes of *"At Last"* drifted through the ballroom, smooth and rich and so perfect it almost made her laugh.

Jace placed one hand at her waist, the other catching hers. His palm was warm, steady. Her breath hitched, just slightly, as the first few steps pulled them close.

"You do know," she whispered, "this is how rumors start."

He leaned in, lips brushing just beside her ear. "Then maybe I should go ahead and give them something real to talk about."

Before she could respond, he turned them with a confident pivot, guiding her across the dance floor in one smooth motion. Her heels slid effortlessly with his steps, and suddenly—

They were in full view.

Directly in front of the cameras.

The lights caught them instantly, flashes erupting in rapid bursts.

And there, with no hesitation, Jace kissed her.

It was intentional. Unapologetic. Yes, the world was watching, but that wasn't why he did it.

He kissed her because he wanted to. Because she wanted him to. Because whatever this was between them, it didn't need hiding anymore.

It wasn't for show.

But he didn't mind if the world saw it.

Dozens of cameras clicked. A sea of light and sound pressed in around them. But in that moment, none of it mattered.

Only the feel of her lips.

Only the way her hand gripped his lapel.

Only the truth between them.

Chapter Thirteen

♥

Spencer curled her feet beneath her on the patio chair, holding the stem of her wine glass lightly between her fingers. The sky over the Pacific was fading into streaks of gold and lavender. A breeze came off the water, soft and cool against her skin.

Dinner had been... more than good. It had been thoughtful.

Simple, but elegant. Pan-seared sea bass with a lemon-herb butter. Wild rice pilaf dotted with toasted almonds and a hint of dried cranberries. Grilled asparagus with lemon zest, bright and crisp without a single trace of garlic or onion. Almost as if he created the menu in hopes of a goodnight kiss or two.

Not that she was complaining. Spencer had spent much of the day thinking about a replay of those kisses herself.

"I thought about making pasta," he said as he settled into the chair across from her. "But fresh pasta's more fun to make together."

His smile wasn't practiced. It was warm. Maybe a little hopeful.

"Maybe next time."

The words settled in her chest like the first line of a new story. One she wasn't sure she deserved to write, but desperately wanted to. With him.

"I'm kind of shocked," she said, glancing toward the table where their plates sat empty. "I don't think I've ever seen an article that mentioned Jace Rose can cook."

Jace smiled and reached for his own glass. "That's because Jace Rose can't."

She looked at him, one brow raised.

He leaned back in his chair, legs stretching toward the low patio wall, one ankle crossing over the other.

"Jace Rose relies on catering and takeout," he said. "He books restaurants three weeks out and pretends that counts as planning ahead. But Jason Rhodes? He can cook. Clean. Fix a leaky faucet, then perfectly match the colors and textures of the throw rug so no one knows there ever was a leak."

"My father was... let's just say there's a reason I don't call him 'Dad.' He didn't earn the title. He worked, she took care of the kids. And the house. And all of his personal needs. And she was required to look like a runway model while doing it. He thought he was a good man because he kept a roof over her head, money in her accounts, and the bruises where they couldn't be seen."

He paused, letting the wine swirl in slow, silent circles.

"When he left us, my mother was determined that her son would be a real good man, not the imitation Chris Rhodes was. She figured the best way to raise a good man was to raise a good woman first. She taught me how to do laundry, fold a fitted sheet, and cook dinner without setting off the fire alarm. Basically anything that in the seventies and eighties was considered 'woman's work,' Mom made sure I could do. She used to say she was gonna make a good wife out of me."

He smiled, but there was something behind it.

"I don't think she ever expected I'd still be doing it all alone at thirty."

There was something tender in the way he said it. Not bitter. Just honest.

"When I stepped away from the spotlight, I needed something to occupy my time. I focused on food, taught myself how to make more elaborate dishes, took classes for the stuff I couldn't pick up on my own." He looked up at her and smiled. "I just don't often have anyone to share my skills with, other than Mom and Heather. And they're always happy they didn't have to cook anything. So I'm never really sure how good I am."

Spencer let the silence linger, then said quietly, "You're very good. She raised a good one. For what it's worth." She paused. "Jason."

His eyes met hers. "You know, I don't think I have ever had a girl I was dating call me Jason before. I've never been comfortable enough to share that part of my life with anyone."

She took another sip of wine, then set the glass down. Her fingers rested lightly on the arm of her chair, steady and sure, even as her pulse quickened. But she didn't look away.

"And if you can trust me enough to let me meet Jason..."

She drew a breath, shoulders lifting slightly before settling again.

"It's nice to meet you, Jason Rhodes."

She extended her hand across the space between them, her smile soft but just a bit unsteady.

"I'm Angie Smith."

He didn't say anything right away. Just looked at her hand for a second. Then he reached out and took it, a slow smile spreading across his face.

"Hi, Angie."

She smiled a bit wider. "No one calls me that, except back home in Eaton Rapids. And when I visit my parents in Florida."

"Eaton Rapids? Where's that?"

"Michigan," she said, her voice a mix of pride and resignation. She picked up the wine glass again, more to have something in her hands than anything else. "Just south of Lansing. If you blink at the wrong moment, you'll miss the whole thing, except the river. That sticks around, and not always in good ways."

He nodded. "That explains the East Lansing thing," he said. "I thought it was a strange place to premiere a movie."

"I'm a Michigan State grad," she said proudly. "Class of 1998. I wanted the first showing there as a thank you to those who first believed in me and supported my dreams."

"Eaton Rapids is a small town, with more cows than people. And the people have long memories. Doesn't matter how much success I have, they just see the same little girl, with her nose in a book and her head in the clouds. They never really thought I'd make it as an author. That's not the kind of success that comes from Eaton Rapids."

"So how does Angie Smith become Spencer Callahan? One name sounds like she lives down the block and makes banana bread. The other sounds like she wins Pulitzers before breakfast."

She let out a soft laugh. "Hey now, I make a killer banana bread. And I'll eat a few thousand breakfasts before I win a Pulitzer, no matter what name's on the dust jacket."

He grinned, but didn't push. Just waited.

She swirled the last sip of wine in her glass, her smile fading into something quieter.

"My first agent—yes, there was one before Nora. Less overprotective, not nearly as competent—she loved my writing, but not the name. She said Angie Smith was too plain, too ordinary to sell books. She said I needed something to make my books stand out on the shelf. I told her I wanted to let my work speak for itself, and she laughed. 'Honey, I believe people will love your work. But you need a name on the cover that makes them want to pick it up. Angie Smith just won't cut it.'"

She paused to take a sip, finishing her wine.

"Spencer was my mom's maiden name," she said. "Callahan was my grandmother's. I grew up listening to their stories. Mom read to me when I was sick. Grandma made up better endings when the ones in books didn't feel fair enough. They were the reason I first picked up a pen. So when it came time to put a name on a cover, it felt right to use theirs instead of mine."

She flashed him a quick grin. "And I liked the idea that people wouldn't know if they were reading a book written by a man or a woman, unless I wanted them to know."

"So I'm not the only one you threw off with that, huh?"

Spencer chuckled. "Not even close."

"So what do you prefer, Angie or Spencer?" Jace asked. "For me, it's not a big difference. Mom called me Jace from the time I was a baby. She didn't start using Jason until the rest of the world started shortening it. She wanted to keep something of me for herself."

"I like that," Spencer said, staring out toward the horizon where the sun was beginning its slow descent into the Pacific. "That someone wanted to keep that little piece of you. I'm Angie whenever I go home, and Spencer everywhere else. I like it that way."

She focused on the shifting sky, the changing light. She couldn't quite bring herself to look at him as she added, quietly, "Most of the time, I'd rather forget about Angie Smith. She's not one of my favorite people."

Jace was quiet for a long moment, eyes tracing the line where the ocean met the sky. Then he turned, his voice low. "When you said those things in *Fighting Gravity* didn't happen to you... did you mean they happened to Angie? And Spencer just watched it all happen from a distance?"

She let out a breath, part laugh, part sigh. "I wish." Her eyes stayed on the water, even as the shimmer of it blurred. "That would mean it wasn't my fault."

Slowly, she turned to face him. "But it was my fault. Angie's fault. She failed someone who trusted her, and I don't know how to forgive her for that. When I'm Spencer, I don't have to carry it around. I don't have to think about it every day." She swallowed against the emotion in her throat threatening to choke out her words. "When I'm Spencer, I can almost convince myself that I deserve to be happy."

Jace didn't answer right away. He didn't try to fill the silence. When he did speak, his voice was steady, almost quiet enough to be lost in the breeze. "You don't have to tell me. But if you ever want to... I'm here."

She looked at him then, really looked. And after a long moment, she reached for her empty wine glass.

"If you're sure you want to hear it... I'm going to need more than one glass. One glass won't get me through this story."

"I've got wine," he said. "Will you be okay alone here while I step inside?"

"No," she said. Then, quieter, "But it's fine." She tried to smile. "I'm an author. I'm never really alone. My characters are always with me."

He returned with two bottles tucked under his arm and a pair of clean glasses clinking lightly in his hand.

"I wasn't sure what mood we were drinking for—brooding or bravery—so I brought both." He set the bottles down with a soft thud. "Pinot Noir if we're going deep. Riesling, if we need to remember the world still has sweetness in it."

She didn't even glance at the white. "Pinot."

He poured two generous glasses. As he handed her one, their fingers brushed, lightly, unintentionally, but it lingered in the air between them.

She took the glass, held it for a beat. "I did forget the world had sweetness in it," she said softly. "Until I met you."

Jace's gaze caught hers and held. Then he lifted his glass. "To remembering the sweetness."

She clinked her glass gently against his. "And forgetting the sour."

They drank in silence. Not to fill it—but to honor it.

Chapter Fourteen

♥

A cool gust came in off the water, lifting the hem of her dress and brushing a shiver up her spine. Jace noticed.

"Hang on," he murmured, setting down his glass.

He crossed to the fire pit and crouched beside it, flicking the ignition and adjusting the flame until a steady glow bloomed into warmth. The orange light cast flickering shadows across his face, softening every line.

She watched as he returned, blanket in hand. Without a word, he draped it gently over her shoulders, his fingers brushing the curve of her neck as he did.

Instead of sitting back down in his chair, she shifted—just enough to make space. She tucked her legs to the side, turned toward the fire, and patted the cushion beside her. The gesture was small, but unmistakable.

He hesitated only a moment before accepting it, sliding onto the sofa beside her. Not too close. Not crowding. Just *there*.

She adjusted the blanket to drape between them, then looked down at the wineglass in her hand.

When she hesitated to begin, Jace said, "You don't have to tell me anything, you know. You can change your mind and keep the story to yourself."

"I've already told much of it," she said. "It's where the idea for *Fighting Gravity* came from. Those characters...Cassie and Mia...they are real. Or, mostly real. They were best friends, from the moment Mia's family moved into the house next door to Cassie when they were seven. Back then they weren't Cassie and Mia. They were Andi and Angie."

Jace was silent for a moment, processing. Then, softly:

"If the friendship was real... does that mean the rest was, too? The abuse... the drugs... the suicide attempt?"

She didn't look at him right away. Just stared into the fire, her fingers tightening slightly around the stem of her glass.

"Not all of it happened the same way," she said finally. "But yes. Enough of it did."

She exhaled slowly. "Andi was brilliant. Kind. Fiercely loyal. And talented." She smiled, the flickering firelight dancing off her eyes. "She's the one who should be in the spotlight. It should be her name in lights, not mine. But her parents... They trusted the wrong person, and he took advantage of their little girl." She lifted the wine glass to her lips, draining it in one drink. "Uncle Richard. I still don't know if he was really her uncle or just a friend they felt deserved that title."

Spencer paused, taking a few deep breaths to steady herself. When she spoke next, her voice was full of bitterness. Anger. Hatred. "She was eleven. ELEVEN!! What kind of a man looks at an eleven-year-old child and gets aroused? And what sort of a parent believes him over their daughter when she describes what he did to her? At that age, how would she have even known about those things if he hadn't touched her that way?"

She set the empty glass down with a sharp, controlled motion. Too sharp. A thin web of cracks spread across the base, nearly invisible in the firelight.

Spencer didn't notice.

Her jaw clenched like she was trying to swallow the scream that still lived at the back of her throat.

Jace saw it. Said nothing. Just reached over with quiet care and moved the glass out of her reach, replacing it with his hand instead.

Jace didn't speak right away. He didn't rush in with comfort or platitudes. He just reached over, slow, and steady, and wrapped his fingers around hers. No words—just warmth, anchoring her to the present.

"You were a kid too," Jace said, his voice rough with emotion. "It wasn't your job to stop it. It was theirs. The people who failed her weren't eleven or twelve or fifteen. They were adults. They knew better."

"I know," she said quietly. "And I have a whole reservoir of bitterness and unforgiveness for them, too."

She reached for the bottle of Pinot, then paused as Jace quietly held out a fresh glass.

She didn't ask where it came from. Just took it.

Refilled. Held it in her hands without drinking. Fingers curled around the stem like it might hold her together.

"He ended up going to prison," she added, "but not for what he did to her. Something completely unrelated. Forged checks or something. And her parents?" She gave a humorless laugh. "They still visited him. Wrote him letters. Sent him money. They ignored everything she was going through... and supported *him*."

Jace let go of her hand and gently placed his palm against her back, rubbing slow circles near the base of her spine. Spencer leaned into the touch, letting her shoulder brush his, the tension in her body softening for the first time since starting her story..

"When we went to college," she said after a long pause, "that's where the fiction started. I created Max out of nothing. He's the friend I wish Andi had. The friend I wish I had been."

"So that frat party never happened?"

Spencer shook her head. "No, it happened. Just not the way I wrote it." Her voice cracked as she added, "It was my idea to go. If I hadn't talked her into it..."

She looked away, blinking hard, tears welling too fast to catch.

"Hey," Jace said softly. "Whatever happened there—it's not your fault. Spencer, look at me."

When she didn't move, he reached out, his fingers gentle beneath her chin, guiding her face back toward his. The pad of his thumb swept across her cheek, catching a tear before it fell.

"You should have been able to go to a college party without fearing for your safety. You didn't do anything wrong."

She flinched, a breath catching like a sob. "That's the point." Her voice rose, sharp and hoarse. "Jace, I didn't do anything."

She pulled away slightly, not from him, but from the weight of the memory pressing down.

"Someone spiked my drink. I saw the white powder swirl in the punch. I knew something wasn't right, but I'd already had just enough that I couldn't move fast enough. I looked across the room and saw her. Saw the rolled dollar bill passed into her hand. The guys who brought it weren't even trying to hide it."

She choked on the next words.

"By the time I could make my legs work and get to her... it was too late."

Her voice dropped, hollow now.

"She went from pot to cocaine that night. Within a year, she was dead."

She looked at him then, really looked—and Jace saw it. The haunting heartbreak in her eyes. The kind that didn't fade with time. The kind that settled in and made a home.

"I wasn't even there when she died," she whispered. "She was alone. In our dorm room. But I was the one who found her."

She swallowed hard, and her voice went flat, cold with the kind of hurt that had been carried too long.

"And don't say it's not my fault. Because after hearing her parents scream at me for ten years that I killed their daughter... I won't believe you."

Jace didn't answer.

He didn't try to fix it. Didn't rush in with comfort or contradiction. He just sat there, shoulder to shoulder with her, until the silence cracked and gave way to quiet, helpless sobs.

She folded forward, and he caught her. Pulled her against him, arms strong and steady as she shook with the weight of everything she had never let herself say.

He held her. Let her cry. Let her break.

Only when her breathing began to slow, when her body had softened, exhausted against his, did he speak. His voice was low, steady. No judgment. Just truth.

"I won't try to change your mind," he said. "I wasn't there. I didn't live it. I get why you wouldn't believe me."

A beat passed. His hand moved gently across her back, not urging, just grounding.

"But I will ask you this... why would you believe them?"

She didn't move, but he felt the breath she caught.

"These are the same people who let someone into their home to hurt her. Who didn't believe her when she told them. Who cared more about his prison sentence than the trauma he left behind. So tell me, Spencer..."

He let the question hang.

Then, quieter... "Why would you believe anything they have to say about her?"

Another breath. Still no answer.

"Or about you?"

Chapter Fifteen

The water had gone lukewarm, but he didn't stop washing. It gave his hands something to do. His mind, too.

Outside, the fire pit still flickered, casting faint golden light against the glass doors. Spencer was curled on the sofa, wrapped in the blanket he'd brought out earlier, her breath finally steady after hours of unraveling.

He hadn't known what to expect when she started talking. But he hadn't expected that.

Not the weight of it. Not the *honesty*.

Not the anger he felt at parents he'd never met. Parents who made his wife-beating father appear almost saint-like.

He rinsed another wineglass, set it carefully in the drying rack. The kitchen was quiet except for the soft clink of dishes and the hum of the fridge, allowing his thoughts to rage even louder in his head.

They had one job. One. To protect their daughter. And because they'd failed, two lives had been destroyed.

And they had the nerve to blame Spencer for their failure?

He plunged his wash rag into the sink, holding it there, wishing he could hold the parents' heads under that water instead.

Then he felt her.

Arms slipping around his waist. A kiss against his shoulder. Light, but enough to send a thrill through his spine. Enough to bring him back to this night, this moment, and what he could do now—what he *would* do—to protect her.

She rested her cheek against his back and whispered, "Thank you."

He felt her arms tighten around him, her cheek still resting against his back.

"Thank you," she whispered again.

"For what?" he asked, his voice low. "I just listened."

She held him tighter. "That's just what I needed. Someone to listen."

He stood still, letting her words soak in.

"What I wrote... it took me back there. And then when Nora sold the film rights..." Her breath caught a little. "I had to do the screenplay. I didn't trust anyone else to tell Andi's story. But it took me back there again. All of it."

He turned, wet hands and all, and reached for her, pulled her gently into his arms.

She didn't resist. She melted into the space he offered, arms wrapping around his waist, forehead pressed to his chest.

"But every time I wrote a line for Max," she murmured, "the guilt felt heavier."

Jace's hand moved to the back of her head, fingers threading lightly into her hair.

"Because he was who you wanted to be," he said.

She nodded against him.

"Andi deserved someone like Max," she whispered. "She deserved so much more than me."

Jace held her tighter, his hand still cradling the back of her head.

"She deserved you, too," he said quietly. "Both the version of you that existed back then, who did all she could. And the woman standing in my kitchen right now, who would move heaven and earth for her friend's memory."

Spencer didn't speak, but he felt the way her fingers curled tighter into his shirt.

"You carry so much of that pain like it's yours to keep," he continued, voice low. "But you don't have to carry it alone. You deserve someone who can hold some of that weight for you. And if just listening helped even a little..."

He paused, brushing a strand of hair behind her ear. "Then I'm glad I was here."

She looked up. The tears were still there, but her gaze was steadier now.

"You're working your way into my heart, Spencer. Fast. And seeing you like this, hurting, blaming yourself, it makes my chest feel like it's caving in."

He leaned in, not quite a kiss, just close enough that she could feel the warmth in his breath, the steadiness in him.

"I don't need you to be okay all the time," he said. "I just need you to know that it's okay for you to not be okay with me."

She looked up at him, eyes still rimmed in red, but something new flickering underneath. Something soft, and sure.

"The funny thing is," she said, her voice barely above a whisper, "after knowing you for only a week... I feel more okay than I have in years."

Jace didn't get the chance to respond.

Because she kissed him.

Really kissed him.

Her body pressed into his as her hands slid up his arms, slow and searching, over the curve of his shoulders and to the base of his neck. Her fingers threaded into his hair, pulling him closer, anchoring him to her like he was the only solid thing left in the world.

He answered with a low breath against her lips, one hand at her waist, the other splayed between her shoulder blades, holding her like she was something precious and fragile and burning all at once.

The kiss deepened, not urgent, but undeniable. Years of silence and guilt giving way to something real. Something new.

When the kiss finally broke, their foreheads rested together, breath mingling in the quiet warmth of the kitchen.

Jace let out a low exhale, smiling. "Wow."

She smiled too, still catching her breath. "Yeah."

He laughed softly. "That was one hell of a first kiss."

She blinked, pulled back just enough to look up at him. "What do you mean first kiss? Did you forget about the kisses last night?"

He grinned. "No. I remember. That was Jace and Spencer."

He leaned in again, brushing his lips over hers, softer now, slower.

"This," he whispered, "is Jason and Angie."

She closed her eyes, her heart catching in her throat. The sentiment hit home, but still, she shook her head, gently, with a smile.

"No," she said quietly. "Not Angie."

She opened her eyes and met his, steady and sure.

"Angie's still scared somewhere... still not ready to believe she deserves to be happy."

She reached up, her fingers grazing his cheek.

"But Spencer? She's happy enough to admit that she's falling hard for you."

Jace didn't speak. He didn't need to.

He kissed her again, telling her without words that maybe he was falling, too.

And when she reached for his hand, lacing their fingers together, he didn't ask where they were going. He just followed.

□□□

Sunlight spilled across the sheets in quiet streaks of gold.

Spencer blinked awake slowly, the room coming into focus one soft line at a time, the open window, the curtain shifting with the breeze, the familiar scent of coffee drifting faintly from somewhere nearby.

And the warmth.

Not just from the sun or the comforter that smelled faintly of his sandalwood and citrus cologne.

But from the arm draped across her waist. The soft rise and fall of breath behind her. The steady rhythm of someone else still asleep.

Jace.

She let her eyes close again, just for a moment, waiting for the guilt to come, like it always did.

But it didn't come.

This wasn't the first time she'd woken up in someone's bed after too much wine and too many emotions. She'd been here before, seeking comfort, escape, a way to quiet the noise in her head.

But this time was different.

Jace wasn't a distraction. He wasn't some stranger she'd used to feel something else, or nothing at all.

He was... *Jace.*

And there was no wave of panic. No flood of regret. Just stillness. Quiet. And something dangerously close to joy.

Her fingers brushed the sheet beside her, still rumpled, still warm, and she smiled, small and real.

Then she tried to move.

And realized she couldn't.

Between the sheets twisted around her legs and the arm slung across her waist like a weighted anchor, there was no graceful way to escape. Not that she wanted to. Not really. But the realization made her laugh quietly into the pillow.

Trapped. In the best possible way.

She turned her head slightly and pressed a soft kiss to his arm, just below the curve of his bicep.

He stirred, just enough to tighten his hold on her.

"You're not thinking of leaving, are you?" he murmured, his voice still thick with sleep.

She smiled again, eyes still closed, and nestled closer into the curve of his body.

"No, Jace," she whispered. "I was just thinking how very much I *don't* want to leave."

He smiled against her shoulder and nuzzled closer, his breath dancing over her skin, warm and steady.

"Good," he murmured, pressing a kiss just below her ear. "Because I don't want to let you go."

A pause. A breath.

"Like, ever."

Her heart tripped in her chest, but not in fear. Not in panic. Just... awe.

She didn't answer right away. Just let herself breathe him in. The scent of his skin. The weight of his arm. The feeling of belonging. It was unfamiliar, but not unwelcome.

And in that moment, she believed him.

So she reached for his hand beneath the sheets and laced their fingers together.

Not as a promise. Not yet. Just enough to say, *Me too.*

Chapter Sixteen

♥

The diner was tucked just off the beach. One of those blink-and-you'll-miss-it places with chipped mugs, soft R&B playing low, and the kind of pancakes that could ruin you for life.

Jace slid into the booth first, and Spencer followed, still barefoot in sandals, her hair pulled up in a hasty knot. She wore one of his soft black T-shirts, knotted at the hip, and his flannel shirt tied casually around her waist. Her skirt from the night before had been swapped for a pair of lounge shorts, rolled at the waistband and clearly not hers, but she didn't seem to care.

And Jace? He couldn't stop looking.

He'd always thought the "morning-after-in-his-clothes" thing was just a guy fantasy made up for music videos and sitcoms. But now, watching her fiddle with the sugar packets, sleeves pushed up, her skin glowing in the morning light?

Yeah. Okay. He got it.

Their hands found each other almost without thought—his thumb tracing lazy circles over her knuckles on the table between them.

"I think I want to write something new," she said suddenly, between sips of her coffee. "Something funny. Maybe romantic. With, you know... a happy ending."

He raised a brow, amused. "Spencer Callahan, writing a rom-com? Does Nora know?"

Spencer laughed. "Hey, she repped my first four books for me. Those were too sugary-sweet to be true rom-coms. She knows I can write happy."

He grinned and tightened his fingers around hers. "I like it. You've earned a little happy."

She smiled, soft and real. "Yeah. I think I have."

"You've helped me find that happy, Jace."

She sipped her coffee, then looked at him over the rim of her mug, a playful spark dancing in her emerald eyes. She tilted her head slightly. "Even if you aren't as big as the ocean."

He chuckled. "I didn't hear any complaints last night."

She leaned in, her lips brushing his in a slow, sultry kiss that made it very clear she was still thinking about all they'd done last night.

When she pulled back, her voice was low. "Shall we try again? See if I can find something to complain about?"

He chuckled, leaning in just enough for her to feel the heat in his voice. "Only if you promise not to fake a single complaint."

She leaned across the table, then whispered in his ear, close enough that her lips brushed against his skin, "Just don't make me have to fake the compliments, either."

He blinked. Sat back. Opened his mouth to respond, then closed it again. Spencer laughed into her mug, clearly pleased with herself.

Their waitress slowly approached their table then, giving Jace a brief reprieve.

She was young—maybe nineteen, maybe twenty—and trying very hard to look casual as she tucked a loose strand of hair behind her ear and reached for her notepad. The name on the badge pinned to her apron read "Brianna."

"Hi, uh... sorry for the wait. Are you ready to order?"

Her eyes flicked toward Jace, then back to Spencer. Then to Jace again. Then back to Spencer.

Her hands trembled just slightly as she gripped her pen.

Spencer took pity. "Yeah, we're ready. I'll have the avocado toast with extra lemon, bacon—extra crispy—and another coffee when you get the chance."

Jace raised an eyebrow at her, then turned to the waitress. "Cinnamon roll French toast, extra bacon, and hashbrowns."

He paused, glanced sideways at Spencer, then added with a smirk, "Because breakfast is more than unseasoned guac on crispy bread."

Spencer kicked him under the table, gently, and gave the waitress a playful shrug. "Ignore him. He's just bitter because I got the first zinger."

Brianna gave a small, almost startled laugh, then nodded quickly. "I'll get those right out."

She turned and walked briskly toward the kitchen, still not quite looking at either of them directly.

A few minutes later, their food arrived, piled high and smelling like heaven. They dug in between laughs and sips of coffee, conversation flowing easily.

They talked about everything--high school embarrassments, childhood dreams, her ridiculous fear of bats, his failed attempt at a food truck right after his boyband days. Nothing heavy. Nothing hard. Just life. Just learning about one another.

They'd barely finished their meals when Brianna returned to top off their coffee—again.

Her hands didn't quite stop shaking as she poured, and she hadn't made eye contact since she dropped off their food.

Jace smiled up at her as she finished refilling his mug. "Thanks, Brianna."

She nervously tucked a strand of hair behind her ear. "Y-You're welcome."

She practically bolted after that.

Spencer tilted her head, curious. "Okay, that was the third refill and the fifth walk-by in twenty minutes. I don't think I've ever had such good service."

Jace chuckled. "It happens more often than you think," he said. He sipped his coffee. "When fans realize who I am, either I get great service or I get napkins instead of silverware and a Coke I didn't order—because they're too busy staring to remember how to do their job." He nodded toward their server. "But Brianna's been great. Respectful. Good at her job. Not fawning or flustered. Honestly? That's rare."

Spencer raised an eyebrow. "You think she's so attentive because she's your fan?" She leaned in slightly. "Jace, she's a baby. Maybe her mom is a fan of yours."

He gave her a mock-offended look. "Are you calling me old?"

She shrugged, lips curving. "Hey, I'm just saying..."

He smirked, voice dropping low. "Maybe we should head back to my place after breakfast. I'll show you how not old I am."

She leaned in, eyes warm. "Promise?"

Jace flagged down the waitress to pay. She approached cautiously, wringing her hands in the front of her apron. "Is there anything else I can get for you?" Brianna asked.

"Oh no, you've been great," Jace said, reaching for his wallet. "I just wanted to thank you for such a pleasant morning. It's rare to get a meal in peace when someone recognizes me."

She looked at him in confusion. "Recognizes you?" she repeated. "I'm sorry. Are you famous or something?"

Spencer nearly spit out her last sip of coffee. "You mean you don't know who he is?" She tried not to laugh too hard. "He was sure that was why you kept coming by to refill our coffee cups."

The waitress shook her head. "I mean, I suppose he does look kind of familiar. But..." He face flushed a bright pink. "It's you I recognized, Miss Callahan."

"Me?" Spencer said, pointed to herself. "You know who I am?"

"Yeah," the young girl said. "I've read *Fighting Gravity* four times. I'm reading it again now to get ready for the movie this weekend. I kept coming over because I wanted to say hello. I just didn't want to make a scene. You two looked really happy. I didn't want to ruin that."

Jace smiled, his gaze fixed on Spencer. "We are happy," he said. "And even though you clearly have questionable taste in music, your taste in literature is impressive." He raised Spencer's hand to his lips, pressing a tender kiss to her fingers. "I don't mind sitting in the shadows, so long as I get to watch her shine."

"Oh, stop it," Spencer laughed. "He is always so dramatic."

Brianna smiled shyly, backing a step away. "Sorry, I didn't mean to interrupt."

"You didn't," Jace said, still holding Spencer's hand. "But now I'm curious. What is it you like so much about the book?"

Brianna hesitated, then gave a small, earnest shrug. "It's not just the story. I mean, the plot's great, but... it's the people. The way they're written. They feel real. Flawed, but still worth rooting for. Like, I don't know... like they existed before the book started and they'll keep living after it ends." She glanced at Spencer, cheeks flushed again. "That's what made me fall in love with it. The characters just... breathe."

Spencer blinked, momentarily lost for words.

Jace glanced at her, pride written all over his face. "Told you. She's the real star."

Brianna ducked her head. "I want to be a writer, too," she admitted. "But I'm not that good. I can spot good literature when I read it. But creating it? That's different. I'll never be as good as you are, Miss Callahan."

Spencer found her voice, soft and sincere. "I wasn't always a good writer myself," she said. "My high school composition teacher would be happy to share how not good I was. And my first novel? Rejected by three agents and five publishers. The version that finally made it to print? That was the eighth complete revision. And *Broken By You* still isn't good for much more than lining a gerbil cage—at least, according to my favorite review."

"Ouch," Jace said. "That was your favorite review?"

Spencer nodded. "It was. I have it framed in my office, above my writing desk. It reminds me why I do this. Because the only way to improve—the only way to make those reviewers eat their words—is to show up every day and write the story that needs to be told."

"So that's what I need to do?" Brianna asked. "Just write each day, and I might become the next Spencer Callahan?"

"Oh, I sure hope not," Spencer said with a laugh. "The world doesn't need the next Spencer. They've already heard my voice. What it needs is the first Brianna."

The three were quiet for a moment, the look on Brianna's face saying she was letting that settle.

At last, Spencer asked, "Do you, by any chance, have your copy of the book with you?"

Brianna's eyes widened. "Oh! It's in my car. I'm waiting to read more on my break."

Spencer nodded. "Go grab it."

"Seriously?"

She laughed. "Yes. I'll sign it."

As Brianna darted out the door, a man in his late fifties emerged from the kitchen—flour on his shirt, a towel tossed over one shoulder. Dodgers cap, sun-weathered face. He glanced toward the door and then to Spencer, recognition slowly dawning.

"You're really her," he said. "Spencer Callahan."

Spencer offered a small, surprised smile. "Guilty."

He took off his cap and scrubbed a hand through his hair. "My daughter—Brianna—she's read that book of yours more times than I can count. She talks about you like she knows you. Says your book has taught her more about writing than any of her teachers ever have."

Spencer's breath caught, but she nodded softly. "That's... the best thing anyone could ever say about it."

The man hesitated, then added, "Look, I keep an old Polaroid in the office—insurance stuff, usually. But would you mind taking a photo with her? I think it'd mean the world to my girl."

Spencer smiled, warm and full. "Of course."

By the time Brianna returned, breathless and clutching the paperback, her father already had the camera ready.

Jace offered to take the photo, waving off the cook's fumbling fingers. "Let the guy with the steady hands handle it."

Spencer pulled Brianna in for a quick side hug, and just before they smiled, Jace snapped it—capturing them mid-laugh instead.

As the picture began to develop, Spencer signed Brianna's book with a thoughtful note:

Brianna—Thank you for loving this story. For letting it matter. Keep telling your own, okay? With love, Spencer Callahan

Brianna clutched the book to her chest. "I will. I promise."

Her dad took the picture with quiet pride.

As Spencer and Jace headed for the door, her fingers slipped into his like they belonged there.

"That," he murmured once they were outside, "was amazing."

She smiled up at him, light still dancing in her eyes. "She reminded me of someone."

"Angie?" he guessed.

"No." Her fingers tightened in his. "Andi."

Chapter Seventeen

♥

The curb at LAX was chaos—car horns, rolling suitcases, families saying too much or not enough. But in the middle of it, Jace stood still, Spencer's suitcase at his side, her hand still in his.

Spencer adjusted her carry-on strap and gave him a soft smile, the kind that didn't quite reach her eyes.

"So..." he said, voice low. "We're really doing this long-distance thing?"

"Unless I can convince you to move to Michigan," she teased.

He chuckled. "Hard pass. I like having feeling in my toes."

"Well then," she said, brushing a wrinkle out of his T-shirt like it mattered, "I guess we are."

His eyebrows lifted hopefully. "You could move to LA."

"It's tempting," she admitted, her fingers lingering on his chest. "But I'm in the middle of a novel. If I change locations now, the voice might shift. The tone. I've got to finish it where it started."

He nodded, but didn't quite let go of her hand. "How fast can you write?"

"Not fast enough." She leaned in a little. "We'll talk again after the New Year."

He tried to keep his tone light. "As long as I don't have to wait that long to see you."

Spencer rose on her toes and kissed him—soft, lingering, full of promises she didn't yet know how to say out loud.

"You won't," she murmured. "Because I can't wait that long to see *you*."

Jace brushed her cheek with the backs of his fingers, eyes memorizing every line of her face.

She gave one last glance over her shoulder before slipping through the sliding glass doors.

He stayed rooted to the sidewalk, hands in his pockets, watching until the crowd swallowed her.

□□□

Spencer leaned her forehead against the window as the plane began to taxi, her eyes fixed on the stretch of coastline slipping farther away beneath the clouds.

Somewhere out there, past the hills and haze, was his house. His studio. Him.

She didn't know if she was actually looking in the right direction, but it felt like she was.

Could this be possible? Was she already missing him?

She wasn't sure.

But one thing, she knew without question.

The impossible had already happened.

Spencer Callahan had fallen desperately in love with Jace Rose.

She smiled.

And she had a sinking suspicion that he just might feel the same about her.

□□□

Spencer landed in Chicago under a sky the color of dishwater and a chill that crept under her jacket before she even made it off the jet bridge.

She hated that her first thought wasn't *I'm back in the Midwest* but *I'm not in his arms.*

Inside the terminal, she followed the crowd toward Concourse F, the droning sound of rolling suitcases and overhead announcements blending into a kind of static. She wasn't tired exactly, but she wasn't awake either. Just somewhere in between, suspended in airport limbo with cracked lips and recycled air stuck in her throat.

She dropped into a cold, hard plastic chair at gate F10 and tugged her sleeves down past her wrists. Her fingers curled instinctively toward the left side of her coat. The hydrangea pin he'd given her—cheap and sweet and entirely too sentimental—was still fastened there, tucked just under the collar like a secret.

She missed LA. Not the city, exactly. Not the traffic or the glare of constant sunshine. She missed *him*. His laugh. The way his palm would settle instinctively on the small of her back, like he could sense when she needed grounding. The way he'd whispered "Stay" into her hair that morning, even though they both knew she couldn't.

Her phone finally connected to the network. It buzzed in rapid succession—first a voicemail, then a chorus of texts.

Four unread. One voicemail.

She swiped through them with a tired smile.

Jace – 9:16 AM PT My hoodie is in your carry-on. In case the plane is cold. Or the Midwest is an Arctic wasteland

Jace – 11:34 AM PT Just realized it's your first time flying home since... the premiere. Does it feel different? Because LA feels different without you

Jace — 12:20 PM PT If your plane doesn't have peanuts, demand satisfaction. You're a published author now. There are standards.

Jace — 1:05 PM PT I already hate how quiet the house is.

The voicemail was timestamped at 12:21 PM.

"Hey. Just checking in. Hoping you're safely over Colorado or Kansas or somewhere flat. Not to sound needy—but I miss you already. I know, it's been what, five hours? That's not even long enough for a slow news cycle. But still. Call me when you can."

She tucked her knees up slightly and balanced the phone on them, thumbs hovering.

She typed.

Spencer — 3:22 PM CT FYI: my peanuts *were* stale. But my seatmate was worse. He snored like a chainsaw in a thunderstorm.

She hit send, half-expecting radio silence. But before she could even pocket the phone—

Jace — 1:23 PM PT Should've let me fly with you. I don't snore. But I *do* cuddle. Expert level.

Her brows lifted. She'd slept beside him. She knew that he did, in fact, snore.

Spencer — 3:24 PM CT Are you seriously just sitting there, phone in hand, waiting for me to text you?

Jace — 1:25 PM PT Define "waiting." Because if I say yes, I sound desperate. But if I say no, I'm lying. And you like me honest.

Jace — 1:26 PM PT And I honestly like you, my beautiful Scribe.

She rolled her eyes, but her heart thumped in traitorous agreement.

Spencer — 3:26 PM CT Flattery won't get you a gate pass, Rockstar.

Jace — 1:27 PM PT Not even if I promise to be waiting at baggage claim? With coffee and the kind of kiss you *write* about?

She exhaled, chest tight.

The PA system buzzed overhead. Her flight was boarding.

Jace – 1:28 PM PT Too much?

She stared at his words for three full seconds before answering.

Spencer – 3:28 PM CT Maybe. But don't stop.

Then she stood, tucked the phone into her pocket, and walked toward the gate.

Her seatmate might suck again. Her feet were already aching. But she'd be back in her own bed tonight.

And if she closed her eyes, she could almost feel him there too.

Chapter Eighteen

♥

Eaton Rapids, Michigan

Spencer curled into the corner of the couch, wrapped in a blanket that still smelled faintly of cinnamon dryer sheets and late-night laundry. A paper bag sat crumpled beside her, half-full of sugar-dusted apple cider donut holes. She took a small bite, powdered sugar clinging to her lip, and reached for the mason jar of cold cider she'd poured just before the call.

She tapped his contact. One ring. Two.

"Hey," he said, voice smooth and familiar. "Tell me you're eating something cozy right now."

She smiled. "Define cozy."

He paused. "Something seasonal. Sweet. Possibly smuggled in a brown bag from a roadside orchard."

She laughed softly. "Okay, psychic."

"Michigan girl, mid-October. Come on. You're probably eating cider donuts in fuzzy socks."

"I am not!" She glanced down at her feet. "I hate fuzzy socks. They feel weird. Like I'm walking on a stubbly face."

His laugh carried through the line. "So you don't like the feel of a stubbly face," he said. "You could have told me that, you know. I would've shaved before kissing you."

"I don't like *walking* on a stubbly face," she clarified. "I rather enjoy *kissing* one. Especially yours."

And I miss it already.

Spencer didn't say that part out loud. She smiled as she thought it, though, mentally counting down the days until she could kiss him again.

She could picture him now, standing barefoot in his kitchen, fresh from the shower, wearing nothing but a pair of shorts and a towel slung over his shoulder. Spencer tried to capture that visual in her mind. Purely for research purposes, of course. Jace would make an amazing hero in her next fictional romance.

He was already turning into the perfect hero in her real-life one.

"And I may have bought more than just donuts at that roadside orchard stand," she told him, trying to shake off the warmth his imagined image sent through her. "There may or may not be a package crossing three time zones to reach this guy I met a couple of weeks ago."

"Two weeks," Jace repeated, voice low and husky. "Is that really all it's been? Spencer, I feel like I've always known you."

She didn't know how to respond to that.

Because she felt it, too.

She felt it in the way his voice wrapped around her like the blanket on her shoulders. In the way her breath caught when she pictured him barefoot and smiling, standing in his kitchen across the country, saying things no one had ever said to her and meaning every word.

But if she said what she was thinking—that he filled a hole in her heart, in her life, that she hadn't even realized was just waiting for him—would she sound too much like one of her own characters?

So instead, she took a slow breath, pressed her fingertips into the curve of her cider jar, and said softly, "The best two weeks of my life."

There was a pause on his end. Not long. Just long enough to feel like something settled between them.

"How does it feel?" he asked, voice gentler now.

She blinked. "How does *what* feel?"

"To be Angie again. After all the lights and cameras and headlines about Spencer Callahan."

She leaned her head back against the couch cushion and stared up at the ceiling. The cider tasted like October. The sugar clung to her fingertips. And his question hung in the air like the last leaf not ready to fall.

"It feels... like I'm still taking off the costume," she said finally. "Like I can breathe again, but I'm afraid if I exhale too hard, the whole thing will vanish. The film. The book. The way people looked at me. Like I'm going to discover that I really don't matter to anyone."

He didn't rush in with reassurance. He just let the silence do what it needed to.

When he spoke, his tone was soft and warm, reaching places of her heart no one had ever touched.

"I liked Spencer Callahan on the red carpet," he said. "But I *love* Angie Smith on a couch in not fuzzy socks, talking to me with powdered sugar on her lip."

Her breath caught. Did he say love? Did he really say *I love Angie Smith*? Because she didn't think anyone had ever said those words before.

At least not about this Angie Smith.

"I hope you really mean that," she said.

"I do," he said softly. "Because that's the woman I fell for."

She reached for another donut. Her fingers were shaking just enough to miss the bag.

"And what about you?" Jace asked, that playful tone back in his voice. "What do you think of the guy who talks far too much and lives in a city that doesn't understand seasons?"

"That guy?" She smiled, heart hammering. "The chatterbox with a stubbly face? I think he's the best part of my crazy life."

Chapter Nineteen

♥

Nashville, Tennessee

The Nashville evening was cool enough for a light jacket, the air carrying the faint bite of late fall. From the rooftop patio above the bookstore where she had signed books and talked about her writing process, Spencer leaned on the railing, her gaze caught by a vase of pale blue hydrangeas near the door.

Jace followed her line of sight. "You've got those in every book you've written. Why?"

She smiled faintly. "They were part of my childhood. There was a row of them marking the property line between my yard and Andi's. And they surrounded this old garden shed we turned into a playhouse. We painted the inside with leftover cans from my dad's garage. The flowers made it feel like our own little world—even though our moms could see us from the kitchen windows."

Her hand skimmed over one bloom. "For the movie, they changed them to roses. Said they were cheaper, easier to get. I hated it. It wasn't just a set detail—it was the heartbeat of the story."

From somewhere down the street, the faint twang of a steel guitar drifted up—a slow, mournful ballad that tangled with the cool night air.

She turned to him, almost breathless. "Sing the song for me."

He hesitated only a moment before he began, low and unpolished, the melody soft between them.

Fading in the silence,
Drowning in the weight of days,
Counting cracks along the ceiling,
Watching time just slip away.

Every mirror told a story
I was too afraid to hear,
Every smile was borrowed,
Every heartbeat laced with fear.

When the last note faded, she asked quietly, "Why don't you want to sing it publicly?"

He looked away, hands in his pockets. "I haven't performed in so long, I don't know who would want to hear me."

"I would," she said. Then, after a breath, "If it ever gets nominated for anything, would you sing it publicly then? For me?"

His gaze met hers, steady. "If the song is nominated for a major award, I'll sing at the ceremony. For you. Because you asked me to."

He stepped closer, brushing a loose strand of hair from her cheek before leaning in. The kiss was gentle at first, almost hesitant, but deepened with the quiet certainty of someone who didn't want to be anywhere else.

When they finally broke apart, the country ballad from the street was still floating on the breeze. He kept hold of her hand, sliding his other arm around her waist, and they began to sway, slow, easy, unhurried, letting the music carry them until the rest of the world faded away.

Chapter Twenty

♥

Eaton Rapids, Michigan

She sat on the floor of her living room, knees pulled to her chest, the cell phone cradled loosely in her hand. The house was still. No music, no TV, just the sound of the clock ticking above the fireplace and the occasional creak of old floorboards settling in the cold.

Her parents had just gotten off the phone. Their voices still echoed in her head.

Stuart wants to send you a box. He said it was full of your writing. Yours and Andi's. We didn't give him your address.

Spencer stared at the phone. She didn't plan to call anyone. But her fingers moved before her thoughts caught up.

One ring. Two.

"Hey, Scribe," Jace said, voice warm and familiar.

Her breath caught. "Hi."

That one syllable was all it took.

"What's wrong?" he asked, immediately.

"Janice Raymond died." Spencer took a deep, steadying breath. "Six months ago. Breast cancer."

"Okay," he said slowly. "Should I know who that is?"

"Andi's mom. She spent years telling me what a horrible person I am, how I let Andi down, and all the ways her death was my fault." She swiped at the tears falling from her eyes, angry at herself for even crying over this. "The last thing she ever said to me was that I should be the one in the grave, not Andi."

"Oh, Spencer. I hope you didn't listen to her."

She scoffed. "Of course I did. I was already blaming myself anyway. Her words...well, they didn't help anything."

"Do you want me to come to you?" Jace asked. "I can be on the next flight."

There was a pause.

"No," she said, hoping her voice sounded convincing. "I'll be okay. I just needed to hear your voice. You don't mind, do you?"

"Oh course not," he assured her. "I'm happy to be here for you, even if it's just over the phone."

Then, gently, "How did you find out?"

"My mom. She called me tonight..." Spencer hesitated, her voice going tight. "Right after she and my dad got a call from Stuart Raymond."

"Janice's husband?"

Spencer nodded, even though he couldn't see her. "Yeah. He found a box in the back of a closet while going through some of her things. It's full of old notebooks and photos and stories Andi and I wrote together in middle school. And he wants to send it to me."

Jace didn't say anything right away.

Finally: "Do you want to talk about it?"

"I don't know." She wiped her nose on the sleeve of her sweatshirt. "I wrote *Fighting Gravity* to put it all behind me. Not that I'll ever forget Andi... I'd never want that. But I told her story so that I could move on. And now..." Her voice caught. "Jace, I'm right back there again. I feel like that scared little girl, and I don't know how I'll ever outrun her."

He didn't speak right away. But he stayed with her in the silence, the way only he could.

He was quiet again, but she could hear the breath on the other end of the line. The way he waited, not filling the space, not rushing to fix it.

"This box," Jace said, choosing his words with care. "Do you know what's in it?"

"I mean, I have *some* idea. Old notebooks, dumb stories we wrote, that kind of thing. But also... I don't know. I don't know if I can read it. I don't even know if I want it."

"Then don't take it," he said gently.

"But it's *Andi's*. It's the last piece of her, something I haven't already lost."

He was quiet for a beat. Then asked, "What are you scared of?"

She didn't answer right away. When she did, it was barely a whisper.

"I'm scared he's going to find out where I am."

His voice dropped. Careful, even. "Spencer, did he ever hurt you?"

"Not physically," Spencer said. "But Stuart Raymond... he threatened me. Oh, he framed it as a joke. He always complained that I was too outspoken, that I wasn't behaving like a proper young lady. And that I wasn't the 'right' sort of friend for his daughter."

She swallowed hard.

"From the time I was fourteen, when Uncle Richard, the man who hurt Andi, was released from prison, Stuart made these offhand comments about how just five minutes alone with Uncle Richard would teach me a woman's 'rightful place.'"

Her voice shook, but she pressed on.

"Jace, he doesn't know I'm Spencer Callahan. He doesn't know I wrote *Fighting Gravity.* I've done a lot of good with that book—I've set up scholarships in Andi's name, supported charities that help girls recover from that kind of abuse. But if Stuart ever found out the kind of money I've made from it…"

"Okay," Jace said, calm and steady. "Then you don't have to take that risk. You don't have to open that door."

She let out a long, shaky breath. "But I kind of want the box. And I hate that I want it."

He didn't hesitate.

"Then have it sent to Nora's office," he said. "That way it doesn't come to your house. You'll have it when you're ready, but you'll still be safe."

Then, quieter but stronger somehow, "And Spencer… you are not that scared little girl fighting this alone. You have me now. And I will never let that man hurt you. Not with words. Not physically. He won't get close enough."

She closed her eyes, let the silence stretch for a moment. She didn't feel fixed. But she didn't feel alone either.

And somehow, that helped.

"Jace?"

"Yeah?"

"You know how you asked me if I wanted you to come?"

"I remember."

"I lied." Her voice caught. "I want you to come."

There was a pause. She could hear the shift in his breathing.

"But I can't ask you to," she added quickly. "I'm leaving in the morning. St. Louis, signing at an indie bookstore, then a speech at a community college."

He didn't speak right away. When he did, his voice was low. "I'm really glad you called."

"Yeah," she whispered. "Me too."

A beat passed.

"It's late," she said softly. "I should try to sleep."

"Okay. But stay on the line, okay? I'll talk to you until you fall asleep."

She curled tighter into herself, the phone still pressed to her ear.

"You don't have to."

"I know," he said. "But I want to."

A long pause.

Then, hesitantly: "Jace?"

"Yeah?"

Her voice was smaller now, almost a whisper. "Will you sing me a lullaby?"

She half expected him to tease her, or gently back away. But he didn't.

There was a soft rustle on the other end. A pause. Then his voice came through, low and warm.

He started humming first—just a melody. One she recognized before he ever reached the words.

Moon River.

Her heart squeezed. Not because of the song itself, but because he *knew* it would soothe her. Because he chose something soft and timeless, something that sounded like safety and home.

And when he finally began to sing—quiet and unhurried—her breath slowed. Her body settled. Her eyes drifted closed. And in that quiet, she knew: *I'm falling in love with this man.*

Somewhere between his voice and the silence that followed, she let go of the fear.

And finally, she slept.

Chapter Twenty-One

♥

St. Louis, MissouriDreaming in Ink Independent Book-store

The line stretched out the door of the indie bookstore, winding past display tables of pumpkin-scented candles and stacked paperbacks with her name on the cover. Spencer smiled for the hundredth time, her cheeks aching in that quiet way they always did after long events. Her hand was beginning to cramp from singing, but she didn't mind.

Not really.

She had turned her phone to silent before the event started. Not because she didn't want to hear from him—she *did*. So much that it made her chest tight just thinking about it. But if she saw his name pop up, she'd get distracted. And if she responded, she'd *disappear* from this moment, from these people who had waited in line to meet her, to thank her, to tell her how a book helped stitch some broken part of them back together.

So for now, she was focused on her work.

She handed a signed copy to a middle-aged woman with bright eyes and trembling fingers. The woman hesitated before stepping away, then leaned forward with the careful urgency of someone sharing something sacred.

"Your book saved my life," she whispered. "I—I used to be addicted. Pills, then worse. And I lost everything. But I got a second chance. My sponsor helped, sure. But mostly... it was Max."

Spencer tilted her head, brows knit gently. "Max?"

"My dog. Maxwell. A little red Dachshund with a crooked tail and breath like garbage." The woman laughed, wiping at one eye. "I used to read to him. Every night. He just curled up next to me, and I swear he understood every word. Especially yours. I think he loved your Max almost as much as I did."

Spencer reached out and squeezed the woman's hand, grounding her in that moment. "I'm so glad you're still here. I bet Maxwell is, too."

The woman nodded quickly, smiled through tears, and moved on.

Spencer took a slow breath, then reached for the next book.

The paper felt cool beneath her fingers. The pen clicked softly into place. She didn't look up right away. Just opened the cover and asked, "Who should I sign this to?"

And then—

A voice. Familiar. Teasing. Warm.

"To my favorite stubbly-faced chatterbox."

Her hand froze mid-letter.

Her eyes shot up, disbelieving.

Her pen froze. The world narrowed to the curve of his smile and the fact that her heart had just vaulted into her throat.

Jace stood on the other side of the table, one hand braced on the edge, the other stuffed casually in his pocket. He wore a hoodie under his jacket, ball cap pulled low, like maybe he hoped not to be noticed. But he couldn't hide that smile.

The one that turned her whole body into electricity.

She stared at him, speechless.

He shrugged. "You said you missed kissing it. I thought I'd better bring the stubble back to you."

Her lips parted. Maybe to laugh, maybe to cry, maybe just to breathe.

"Jace..." she whispered.

And just like that, her carefully constructed public poise cracked. Not in a dramatic way. Just in the quiet softening of her face. The way her shoulders fell. The way the pen slipped from her hand and hit the table with a quiet clink.

"May I?" he asked, nodding toward the line behind him.

Spencer came around the table like gravity had tilted in his direction. Her arms slipped around his neck just as his wrapped around her waist, lifting her slightly off the ground in one smooth pull.

His ball cap, pulled low to hide his face, slipped off with the motion, landing on the carpet beside them.

She whispered near his ear, "You really flew all the way here?"

"You needed me," he murmured, tightening his hold. "Where else would I be?"

Gasps rose from the crowd as their lips met.

One beat of stunned silence soon turned into...

"Oh my goodness, it's him!"

"That's *Jace Rose*! He just—he picked her up!"

Squeals. Scattered claps. A few camera flashes.

It was only a few seconds. Maybe four. Maybe five.

But it felt like forever.

And not long enough.

Jace pulled back just enough to look at her, forehead resting against hers.

"Hi," he said softly.

"Hi," she breathed back.

She barely registered the flashes or the swirl of whispers until a throat cleared sharply behind her.

"Spencer," Nora hissed, stepping forward with her clipboard clutched like a shield. "This is not professional. You have fans waiting!"

Spencer turned her head, blinking like she'd come up for air.

But before she could speak, someone from the line called out:

"It's fine. We're *living* for this!"

"This is like real-life Cassie and Max!"

"I *knew* you were writing about someone!"

Nora looked like she'd swallowed a lemon. "That may be, but—"

"It's okay," Spencer said quietly. Not just to Nora, but to herself. "This matters too."

She turned back to the crowd, cheeks flushed, hands still resting on Jace's arms. "Everyone, this is—"

"We *know* who it is!" someone shouted, laughing. "Hey, Jace! You signing autographs, too?"

He grinned, retrieving his cap from the floor. "Only if Spencer doesn't mind. You all came to see *her*, not me."

That didn't stop the rush.

Suddenly, copies of the film's soundtrack flew off the nearby table. CD cases thumped open, Sharpies waved in the air. A staff member scurried over with a second chair and set it beside Spencer's.

"Mr. Rose," she asked breathlessly, "can I get you anything? A bottle of water, maybe?"

He took the Sharpie she offered, but his eyes were on Spencer.

She was smiling at him—soft, glowing, proud.

"No thanks," he said, dropping into the chair. "I've got all I need right here."

And just like that, the room collectively melted.

Spencer shook her head, laughing under her breath as she turned back to the line. "Okay, okay—romance break is officially over. Who's next?"

But her eyes darted to Jace's again as he leaned in to sign a CD, ball cap resting in his lap now, stubble catching the light.

Because the stubbly-faced chatterbox she'd been missing all week?

He was right there.

And he wasn't going anywhere.

□□□

Nora caught up with her outside the staff restroom, clipboard clutched like a lifeline. "A cross-country booty call? You let him hijack a scheduled event—"

"Stop." Spencer turned, voice calm but edged. "You handle my schedule, not my personal life. And if you talk about him, you'll do it with respect."

Nora blinked. "Spencer—"

"No. I don't care what you think of Jace or the odds. I'm happy. For the first time in a long time. Get on board, or step off the train."

The bookstore manager, Kathy, bustled past with a stack of backlist titles. "We were already having a record day, but now? Sold out of the soundtrack, customers asking for a Valentine's event..." She hummed a familiar tune as she vanished toward the register.

Spencer allowed herself a small, satisfied smile and slipped into the restroom.

Chapter
Twenty-Two

♥

New York City

It had been Spencer's idea to skip the show.

Her final meeting ran late, and her head was still buzzing with edits and timelines. By the time Jace met her on the steps outside her publisher's building, she didn't want spotlights or velvet curtains. She wanted something slower. Quieter. Him.

They ended up at a French bistro in the West Village—a little place with weathered brick walls, mismatched candleholders, and gold-rimmed mirrors that made the room feel like a memory. It smelled like roasted garlic and warm butter, and when the hostess led them to a small table in the corner, Spencer exhaled for the first time all day.

They shared crusty bread with salted butter and a bottle of red wine Jace pretended to know something about. He ordered steak frites. She went for the roasted chicken, bathed in a tarragon cream sauce so good it made her close her eyes on the first bite.

"This place is perfect," she murmured. "How did you even find it?"

He smiled. "Guy in my old vocal coach's building used to take every one of his dates here. Said if the lighting didn't make her fall in love, the mousse would." He leaned over and whispered conspiratorially, "Though I think he was less interested in having her fall in love than fall into bed."

"And you?" she asked, stealing one of his fries. "Which are you hoping I'll fall into?"

He winked, settling back into his seat. "Can't I have both?"

They were halfway through dinner when it happened. At the next table over--one not quite in the middle of the room, but in a position where ever diner could see it--a man in his twenties pushed aside his dessert plate, cleared his throat, and pulled a small velvet box from his jacket pocket. The woman gasped before he even opened it. Tears followed. The room quieted. Then, slowly, the clinking of forks gave way to applause.

Spencer clapped too, gently, eyes bright as she leaned toward Jace. "I love that she didn't see it coming," she said. "That's the best kind of love. The kind that sneaks up on you. Like ours."

"Is that what you'd want?" he asked, nodding toward the young couple. "A public proposal? Or something more quiet and private?"

"As long as it's the right man asking," she said thoughtfully, "I don't think the setting matters. When I write a proposal, it's usually wildly romantic and a bit over the top." She shrugged. "Readers eat it up. But that's not what I want, really. I just want something heartfelt. I want to know he means it when he asks. Call me old fashioned, but I think marriage should be forever. As long as that is what he has in mind, that he wants to spend forever loving me and being loved by me, that's all that matters."

"Not that I've ever even been close," she added. "There's never been anyone in my life who mattered enough for me to consider forever." *Until you,* she added silently.

He didn't respond right away. He reached for his half-full wine glass, lifted it to his lips, then put it down without taking a sip. His gaze went back to the young couple, though Spencer saw the faraway glint in his eyes. "There was for me." The words were so soft, so quiet, Spencer wasn't sure he'd spoken at all.

"What?" she asked, her smile softening.

He cleared his throat. "A girl I thought I'd spend forever with. We met when I was twenty. I proposed two years later. Not even a year after that, it was over." He turned to Spencer and smiled—sadly, but not bitterly. "Though you probably know all about that. The entire world does. It happened in spring '98. When Inferno was big and then... we weren't."

"That's when I graduated from MSU," Spencer said softly. "Andi had been gone two years by then. I was heavy in the grief of not having her with me. I didn't pay much attention to the world around me... not even my favorite boy band. Sorry."

Jace laughed under his breath. "So you missed my National Enquirer nightmare. Lucky you." He picked up his wineglass, took a sip this time. "Please, allow me to relive it for you."

Spencer reached across the table and gently covered his hand with hers. "You don't have to," she said. "Jace, you don't have to tell me if you don't want to."

"Thanks," he said, giving her a quiet smile. "But it's not as ugly as what you trusted me with. If you can share Andi with me, I can share this."

He turned his hand over, lacing his fingers with hers instead. Letting her comfort shift into connection.

"Her name was Courtney," he said. "Though you'll never hear her called that by my sister. If Heather ever talks about her, it's to call her 'Slutney.'"

"Ouch," Spencer whispered, chuckling slightly.

"Harsh? Yeah. But I warned you—don't anger the grizzly bear. Heather didn't like her to begin with, so..." He smiled, thumb brushing the back of her hand. "She already adores you. I don't think you need to worry about earning a rude nickname."

Spencer arched a brow. "Noted. But remind me never to piss off your sister."

"Anyway," he went on, "I thought we were happy. Had no idea we weren't, not until I decided to grab a bag of Doritos and a case of Mountain Dew at the Piggly Wiggly in Savannah." He paused. "I get to the checkout, and there's Kyle Jeffords, my best friend, my bandmate, on the cover of *The Enquirer*."

She blinked. "He wasn't alone, was he?"

Jace nodded. "Nope. He was with someone the magazine dubbed 'Kyle's Mystery Lover'. Her face was turned away from the camera, hand half-covering it, like she didn't want anyone to recognize her." He gave a small, dry laugh. "Little tip, Spencer? If you don't want your fiancé to recognize you on a date with his best bud, *don't use the hand with the custom-designed diamond ring he gave you to hide your face.*"

Spencer winced. "Oh my. That's not even funny."

"I know, right," he said, draining the last of his wine. "But I laughed. Right there at the checkout, as I picked up the rag and added it to my purchase. The kind of laugh that sounds like someone dropped a piano on your chest. Sure as hell felt like one had been dropped on mine."

After a moment of silence, Spencer asked, "What did you do? You don't have to answer that. Obviously, you didn't marry her..."

"I did not," he said, a trace of jaded bitterness in his voice.

"You don't have to say anything more if you don't want."

"But I want to. I haven't talked about this in years, but I want you to know." He raised her hand to his lips, pressing a tender kiss to it. "I want you to know everything about my life, even the dark parts I'd rather forget."

Her gentle smile urged him to go on. "So I took the magazine back to the tour bus, where I found Kyle sleeping in the lounge. Woke him by slapping him in the face with it. Asked if it was true. He tried to deny it, said it was taken way out of context. Might have been able to convince me, too, if Courtney hadn't rushed onto the bus, calling his name in a panic over the photo she had just seen."

Jace leaned back, the weight of it all pressing into the silence between them. The candle on the table flickered, casting soft shadows against his cheekbone.

"That was the end of Inferno," he said finally. "I finished the last two weeks of the tour—barely. Then I walked away. Didn't care about contracts or promoters or loyalty. The other guys thought I should suck it up for the sake of the fans. Said Kyle didn't mean to fall for her. That things... just happen."

Spencer stayed quiet. She knew the power of silence when someone was telling a story they'd buried deep.

"But I couldn't do it," he went on. "I couldn't go on stage night after night acting like nothing was wrong. Pretending it was all normal. Pretending *I* was okay with the way things happened." His jaw tightened. "And when I left—what they said about me in the press..." He shook his head slowly. "Kyle especially. Called me a sore loser. Said I had a big head. That I thought I was the only talented one, and Inferno couldn't survive without me."

Spencer winced. "Ouch."

"Yeah. And the worst part?" He gave a humorless laugh. "People believed him. Fans turned on me overnight. They were mad at *me* for breaking up the band. Not him for breaking my heart. Not her for cheating. *Me*."

He paused, swirling his empty glass out of habit. "My solo album flopped. Not because it was bad—it wasn't. I'd been working on it for over a year. It just... didn't matter. People were angry, and angry people don't buy records."

"And that is why I refuse to answer when anyone asks me when Inferno will get back together. No one wants to know the truth. There will be no reunion until Kyle Jeffods grows a heart—or whatever it is he has that passes for one stops beating."

He looked over at her, the sadness still there, but quieter now. "I'm not mad that they got together. I'm not mad that Courtney chose someone else. She had every right. But I'm still bitter over what she *cost* me. I lost my girl. My best friend. And my career. All in six months."

His voice dipped, barely audible. "Things could've been so different if she'd just told me she wasn't happy. If she'd just... said something. But the way I found out it was over—" He cut himself off, closing his eyes for a second.

"That photo," Spencer finished softly.

He nodded once. "Yeah. That photo."

She didn't say anything for a moment. Just watched him, heart aching in ways she hadn't expected.

"I'm sorry," she said finally. "That all of that happened to you."

His gaze flicked up to meet hers. "I didn't tell you to make you feel sorry for me."

"I know." She offered a gentle smile. "But I'm sorry anyway."

He nodded once. Then reached across the table again, threading their fingers together on the linen-covered surface between them.

"Just promise me," he said, voice low, almost lost beneath the ambient clatter of dishes and soft French music, "if you ever stop being happy... you'll tell me. Don't let me find out by accident."

Her thumb brushed gently across his knuckles. "I promise."

A long pause stretched between them. Not awkward—just full. Full of understanding. Of trust. Of something building that neither of them wanted to name too soon.

Jace leaned back, his tone quiet, almost thoughtful. "Far as I know, Kyle and Courtney are still together."

Spencer tilted her head. "Really?"

He nodded. "Yeah. And I'm not even angry about that." His eyes met hers, steady and clear. "Because if I'd married her... I wouldn't be here with you right now."

Something shifted in her chest—something soft and wide and wordless. She smiled, motioning for the waiter.

"Could we have the chocolate mousse, please?" she asked. "Two spoons."

Then she glanced at the other couple—the newly engaged pair still lost in each other, hands clasped on the white-linen table.

"And send another to their table. On us. And bring their bill, too—quietly."

The waiter nodded, disappearing with a knowing smile.

The mousse arrived in a delicate glass coupe, glossy and dark and elegant in its simplicity. Spencer slid one spoon toward Jace, but he beat her to it, scooping the first bite and offering it to her without a word.

She leaned in, lips closing over the spoon, eyes on his the whole time.

When he set it down, his hand shook just slightly.

She didn't say a thing.

They ate slowly, passing the mousse back and forth in comfortable silence. Every so often, their fingers brushed at the stem of the glass or lingered a moment too long on the spoon. Time thinned and softened, until there was nothing left but candlelight and the unspoken current between them.

As Spencer set her spoon down, Jace tilted his head, watching her with that lazy half-smile that made her stomach flutter.

"You have a bit of chocolate," he murmured, "just there."

He leaned in and kissed it away, lips brushing the corner of her mouth with the barest pressure—gentle, deliberate, devastating.

She didn't breathe until he pulled back.

When the dessert was gone and the check had been settled—quietly, with a nod to the newly engaged couple—they stepped out into the city.

□□□

Outside the hotel, the night was alive—taxi horns, soft laughter, steam curling from vents in the street. The city never paused, not even for moments like this.

Jace reached out and tucked a strand of hair behind her ear, his fingers grazing her cheek like he didn't want to stop touching her.

"Want to come up?" she asked, voice barely above a whisper.

He studied her for a long second. Not just her face, but *her*. Everything. The moment. The meaning.

"Only if you're sure."

She didn't answer with words.

She answered with a kiss, soft, certain, and full of everything she hadn't said.

And when she reached for his hand, he didn't hesitate.

Chapter
Twenty-Three

♥

L *akeland, Florida*

The car rolled to a stop in front of a one-story house draped in fall garlands and Tigers gear. A *Welcome Fall, Y'all!* sign staked in the yard sat beside a giant metal old English D. Jace wasn't sure if that was charming or vaguely threatening.

Spencer reached for his hand. "Hey," she said softly, thumb brushing his knuckles. "Don't worry. They'll love you."

He smiled, a little tight. "Because I brought flowers?"

"No." She kissed his cheek. "Because I do. And they love me."

"You... do?" He said slowly. "You love me?"

She grinned. "Maybe. I don't *not* love you." Another quick kiss. "Come on, Rockstar. Let's do this."

She handed him the bouquet, looped her arm through his, and they started up the walkway. The door opened before they knocked.

"Happy Thanksgiving!" a woman called, wiping her hands on a dishtowel. Jeans, Tigers sweatshirt, no-nonsense expression, and a bright fall leaf clip in her hair. "Oh, it's so good to see you!" She hugged Spencer, then turned to Jace. "You must be Jace. I'm Judy—Angie's mom."

"Nice to meet you, ma'am," he said quickly, offering the flowers.

"Don's in the living room," she said, already steering Spencer toward the kitchen. "And you, missy, are helping peel potatoes. Fancy author or not."

"Mom, I can't leave him alone with Dad," Spencer protested.

Don appeared in the entryway, giving Jace a once-over. "This the boy you brought home? Think he can't handle a little in*terror*gation?"

"The word is interrogation," Spencer said dryly.

"Not the way I do it," Don replied. "Any good Daddy's gonna put some terror into it, whether the date's fifteen or thirty-five."

Spencer mouthed *I'm sorry* to Jace as Judy pulled her into the kitchen.

"Follow me, son," Don said.

The living room was a shrine to Detroit baseball—framed posters, stacks of old VHS tapes labeled *Opening Day '89, AL Pennant '87,* and a bobblehead display that made Jace mildly uncomfortable.

"Mr. Smith, sir. Good to meet you."

Don shook his hand—firm, slow. "You're the boy my Angie brought home."

"Yes, sir."

"If she trusts you to know her as Angie, I suppose I can trust you to call me Don."

He crossed to a small bar, where a signed Al Kaline photo leaned against a bottle of Maker's Mark with a yellowing tag: *To be opened the day the Tigers win the Series again.*

"You want a drink? I've got Bud, Bud Light, and water."

"Bud's great, thanks."

They sat—Don in his recliner, Jace on the sofa between two blue-and-orange pillows.

"Let's talk baseball. You like it?"

"Of course. Can't say I'm overly familiar with the Tigers, but I know about that home run in Game 5 of the '84 Series. Gibson sure knew how to knock them out when needed."

That earned Jace the first crack of a smile. "I was there, three rows behind third base. Gibson owned Goose Gossage that day."

Jace nodded. "My team's always been the Dodgers, so yeah... Gibson's kind of a legend for me, too."

Don studied him. "Alright, Jace Rose. Maybe you're not just pretty hair and eyeliner."

"I haven't worn eyeliner in years," Jace said, deadpan.

Don chuckled once. "Well. At least you're funny."

Chapter Twenty-Four

♥

By the time the turkey hit the table, the house was full. Spencer's mom had swapped her Tigers sweatshirt for an apron that read *Butter Me Up*, and the kitchen smelled like every good memory Jace had ever tried to recreate in a hotel kitchenette and failed.

Carol Anne greeted Judy with a warm hug and a dish towel already in hand. "I brought the stuffing," she announced, holding the casserole dish like it was made of gold.

"Oh, thank you," Judy said. "If I had to make one more starch today, I was going to start throwing spatulas."

Heather barreled in behind her mother, eyes wide. "Oh my gosh—is this Spencer Callahan's actual childhood home? Like, *this* is where she wrote her first book?"

Spencer blinked. "I was seven when I attempted my first book."

"That counts."

"And Mom and Dad didn't move here until three years ago. Sorry to disappoint you, Heather, but I've never written more than an email here."

Heather gasped like it was a personal betrayal. "Well then I need to see *that* house someday. The one where *Chapter One* really happened."

Judy slid a tray of rolls onto the table with a practiced thud. "Let's survive Thanksgiving first."

Don stood at the head of the table, carving fork in one hand, electric knife in the other. "If y'all don't sit down soon, I'm starting without you."

Carol Anne guided Heather toward her seat, still laughing, and Judy herded the rest of them in like it was a team sport. As chairs scraped and plates clinked, Spencer caught Jace's eye and smiled at him in the seat beside her. He looked at her like he was trying to memorize the whole moment, every laugh, every clatter, every chaotic beat of it.

Midway through dinner—somewhere between Don explaining, in excruciating detail, why the Lions hadn't won a Thanksgiving Day game in over a decade, and Heather demanding the secret to Mamaw Smith's sweet potato casserole—Carol Anne smiled across the table at her son.

"You know," she said, casually reaching for the green beans, "this is the first holiday I've spent with you and someone you're dating since... well. Since your boy band days."

Jace groaned. Audibly.

Spencer didn't even try to hide her grin. "You mean since *I* had his poster on my wall."

"Poster?" Judy said. "I remember more than one. You had so many posters of his band in your bedroom that I nearly forgot the color of your walls." She turned to Heather and said, "Yellow, by the way. Her bedroom walls were yellow beneath all those Inferno posters."

"You know, I remember all that Inferno talk," Don said, looking toward Jace. "But I didn't realize that's the band you were in. It sure wasn't Jace that she talked about all the time."

"Dad!!" Spencer felt the heat creeping up her cheeks.

"And that poster over your bed? It seems like that was Sam or Steve..."

Jace nearly dropped his fork as he turned to Spencer. "Really?" he said, not even trying to hide the amusement in his voice. "Steven Grant... I had no idea I was dating one of Grant's Girlies."

"Hey, at least I wasn't part of Harley's Harem!" she said with a laugh.

"Oh, trust me," Heather chimed in, eyes gleaming. "Half my friends were Harley's Harem. And we were in middle school, with no clue what that even meant."

"Don't encourage them," Jace muttered, but he was grinning as he reached for another roll.

"Oh, you shouldn't be embarrassed by it," Heather said. "You did great things with that boy band."

"And even greater things for the mid-90s sales of leather pants," Carol Anne said.

"I'm begging you both to stop talking," Jace muttered, reaching for his wine.

"Do you have *any* idea," he added, directing it at his mother, "how deeply insulting the term *boy band* is to the people who actually lived it?"

Don didn't look up from his plate. "You were boys. You were in a band. Where's the insult?"

Heather cracked up. "He's got you there, Bro."

Spencer leaned in and stole a bite of his mashed potatoes. "It's okay. But I think you turned out to be the best." She dropped her voice to a whisper and added, "And I'd love to see you in those leather pants."

He gave her a flat look, but there was no hiding the slight flush in his cheeks—or the way his hand brushed against hers under the table, just once, like a thank you.

The conversation moved on to Don's favorite subject, and once he started talking about the Tigers chances in the upcoming season, even Jace knew he wouldn't stop anytime soon.

With a smile, he turned to Spencer and said loud enough for only her to hear:

"This is the best holiday I've had in years."

She smiled at him over her wine glass. "Told you they'd love you."

Chapter Twenty-Five

♥

The dishes were mostly done. Or at least being handled by Judy and Carol Anne with military precision and too much laughter for anyone to interrupt. Don and Heather were deep in a debate about which version of *A Christmas Carol* was definitive, their voices drifting through the cracked windows behind them.

Outside, the porch was quiet. Just cool enough for Jace to wish he'd grabbed a jacket—but not enough to move from where he sat beside Spencer on the old porch swing. Their fingers were intertwined, her bare toes curled against the slats, the swing creaking gently beneath them.

"I still can't believe we're in the same city tonight," he said, watching the streetlight flicker at the end of the drive. "And we're not even staying under the same roof."

Spencer gave a soft, rueful laugh. "I know. It feels backwards, doesn't it?"

He leaned his head against hers, the warmth of her hair brushing his cheek. "If I had my way..."

"You'd have your way with me," she finished, smiling against his shoulder.

He turned just slightly, brushing his lips against her temple. "Over and over again."

She laughed softly, tilting her face toward his. "Bold of you to assume I'd let you."

"Bold of you to claim you'd complain," he murmured, eyes flicking to her mouth.

They kissed again, slow, unhurried, and far too short.

When they pulled back, he stayed close. "There's something I should tell you," he said quietly. "I was offered a part in a Broadway show while I was in New York."

Her brows lifted. "Oh?"

"I turned it down."

"Why?"

"Because it's supposed to be an ensemble show, but they wanted to put me alone on the promos. The producers wanted to use my face and my fame, or my infamy, to sell tickets."

"That's... I don't know if it's sad or pathetic, but it's something."

He shrugged. "It's okay. I didn't really want to do the play anyway."

"No?"

"No. I only went to the meeting because it gave me an excuse to be in New York when you were there."

Spencer didn't have time to figure out why hearing that made her heart soar, why it settled somewhere deep, warm, and a little dangerous, before the front door creaked open and Carol Anne stepped out onto the porch.

"Jace? We're packed up. You ready to head out?"

He didn't move. Didn't even look away from Spencer.

"No," he said, turning to kiss her one last time. "Not sure I'll ever be ready to go."

Chapter Twenty-Six

The porch was quiet again.

Spencer stayed on the swing after Jace left, rocking gently with one bare foot against the floorboards. The air was cooler now. Still. Like even the breeze had decided to rest.

The door creaked behind her.

Judy stepped out with two mugs, one coffee, one chamomile, and handed the tea to her daughter before easing down into the other chair.

They sat in silence for a while. Just the swing creaking and the distant murmur of Don arguing with the *SportsCenter* analysts floating through the cracked open window.

"He's sweet," Judy said eventually. "Thoughtful. Funny."

Spencer nodded without looking up. "Yeah."

Judy took a sip from her mug. "You love him?"

Spencer hesitated. Not because she didn't know the answer—but because saying it out loud made it feel more real than she was ready for.

"I don't know," she said softly. "Maybe."

"That's not a no."

Spencer let the swing slow. "It's not that simple."

"No," Judy agreed, "it never is. Especially not for you."

That made Spencer glance over, brow furrowed.

Judy didn't press. She just held her gaze, steady and kind. "I know how hard you hold on, Angie. To things that hurt. To guilt that doesn't belong to you."

Spencer looked down into her tea, watching the steam curl upward.

"You've spent so long convincing yourself you don't deserve good things," Judy continued. "But I need you to hear me when I say—you do. You *do*."

Spencer blinked fast, her voice barely above a whisper. "Sometimes it just feels... wrong. Like I'm not allowed to be this happy."

Judy reached over and took her hand, warm and solid.

"She would want this for you, you know," she said gently. "Andi would want you to be happy. She wouldn't want you to stop living just because she did."

Spencer didn't say anything. But her fingers curled tighter around her mother's.

And the swing creaked softly beneath Spencer as the night deepened, her mother quiet beside her, and the silence settled into something almost like peace.

Chapter
Twenty-Seven

♥

aton Rapids, Michigan

EShe heard the car door before she heard the knock. The porch light caught the snowflakes in his hair, the tips of his scarf already damp from the cold. He didn't bother with a hello. He just stepped inside, dropped his bag, and kissed her like he'd been waiting the fifteen days since Thanksgiving to do exactly that.

Which he had.

The kiss started slow, but didn't stay there. His hands slid under her sweater, her fingers curled in his coat collar, and somewhere behind them, the plates holding two perfectly respectable meatloaf dinners began to cool on the dining room table.

"Hi," she whispered against his mouth when they finally came up for air.

"Hi," he echoed, breathless.

She backed up a step, cheeks flushed, and gestured toward the table. "I, um... picked up dinner. And there's cinnamon rolls. And I lit—well, I was going to light—candles."

Jace glanced at the matchbook beside two unlit tapers, then back at her.

"How attached are you to dinner?"

Her smile curved. "Not at all."

□□□

Jace lay on his side, head propped on one hand, tracing slow circles along her shoulder. The room was dim and soft—pale curtains, a vintage quilt, the faint scent of lavender.

"You know," he said, lips twitching, "this might be the girliest bedroom I've ever been in."

She nudged his thigh with her knee. "Don't pretend you're not into it."

"Oh, I'm into it," he murmured, dragging a kiss from her collarbone to her jaw. "Especially the bedspread. So delicate. So lacy. So... very not hiding anything at all."

She laughed, burying her face in his chest before looking up again, a little more serious. "I'm sorry about the bed, though. I know it's not exactly... spacious."

"It's fine."

"It's not even a queen. The room's too small for anything else, and since it's just me I never thought I'd need more."

He brushed a strand of hair from her cheek, holding her gaze. "You mean you don't bring your groupies back here all the time?"

She grinned. "Nope. You're my first."

His fingers tangled with hers. "And hopefully your last."

Something flickered in her chest at that, quick, warm, and a little overwhelming, but she didn't say anything. Instead, she leaned forward and kissed him again, slower this time, like a promise.

◻◻◻

Just after midnight, they wandered out of the bedroom, still tousled and warm from slow kisses and whispered promises.

Jace padded barefoot into the kitchen wearing nothing but boxer briefs and a T-shirt that might've actually been hers. Spencer followed, wrapped in a short satin robe the color of soft lavender, the tie loose at her waist.

The dining table looked exactly as it had when he arrived—two full plates of meatloaf and mashed potatoes, steam long gone, candles still unlit.

He stopped, staring at the forlorn food like it had personally betrayed him. "This is it? I flew across the country and braved a blizzard for... cold meatloaf?"

"It's barely a snow flurry," Spencer said, brushing past him to open the microwave. "We can reheat it."

He leaned against the fridge. "I cooked for you, remember? Seabass, Spencer. With citrus beurre blanc. I grilled asparagus. Roasted potatoes. Baked bread."

She didn't look back. "And churned butter."

"With herbs."

She slid one plate in to warm. "I loved every bite. But if I tried to return the favor, I'd probably kill you. Louie's felt safer."

"What if Louie's had been closed?"

She turned, deadpan. "Frozen pizza. Boxed mac and cheese. Or ramen. Depending on how much I liked you."

He gasped. "No heirloom tomatoes? No hand-whipped aioli?"

"I don't even have real butter."

The microwave dinged. She handed him the reheated plate, then warmed hers.

He took a bite, then gave her a look that was pure Jace—half teasing, half smitten. "Still not as good as seabass. But at least the company is amazing."

□□□

They ended up curled together on the couch, a fleece blanket over both of them, two reheated cinnamon rolls on a plate between their legs.

"You've got frosting on your finger," Jace said, grinning as he licked it from her knuckle.

"That was mine."

"We're sharing."

She tore off a piece of her roll and brought it to his lips. "Then you can have this, too."

He took it slow—mouth brushing her fingers first, tongue flicking against the sugar, eyes locked on hers. Her breath caught, her robe sliding off one shoulder.

He noticed.

Setting the plate aside, he let his gaze linger on the soft dip of her collarbone. "Suddenly, I have a better idea what dessert should be."

"Oh yeah?" she teased. "And what would that be?"

He slid a hand over her thigh, fingers brushing beneath satin. "Remember when I threatened to have my way with you?"

"Vaguely."

"I think it's time to make good on that promise."

She leaned in, lips just brushing his. "Please do."

And for the rest of the night, cinnamon rolls were the last thing on either of their minds.

□□□

They walked the three blocks to Main Street with gloved hands clasped, their breaths puffing white like little steam engines. Jace wore one of her scarves and a baby-blue knit beanie she'd insisted on—pompom and all.

"This is obscene," he muttered. "No one should live somewhere this cold."

"You're such a California baby."

He narrowed his eyes, but smiled. "You promised me cocoa."

"With extra marshmallows," she said.

"Were you ever a scout?"

"Nope."

"So your honor's questionable at best."

They found a spot along the sidewalk just as the first float rolled past—glowing candy canes and tinsel-strewn teenagers tossing peppermints. A golden retriever in a Santa hat rode in the passenger seat of a vintage red truck. The high school band came next, slightly out of tune but playing like they meant it.

Spencer clapped for every float, waved at every elf, and gasped when the fake snowblower on the hardware store float sent flurries into the crowd.

Jace barely saw the parade. He watched her instead—eyes dancing, face lit with the kind of joy you can't fake. This mismatched little town meant something to her. And somehow, that warmed something in him he thought had gone cold.

She looked up at him, eyes shining, and squeezed his hand like she knew exactly what he was thinking.

And just like that, it hit him.

I love her.

Not lust. Not infatuation. Not the adrenaline rush of sharing a bed with someone whose beauty in sleep rivaled her best prose.

I am totally, irreversibly in love with her.

He didn't say it. Not yet. But he knew. And soon, he'd have to tell her.

Chapter
Twenty-Eight

♥

The smell of sautéed onions and melting cheese still lingered in the kitchen by the time they finished cleaning up. Spencer dried the last plate and passed it to Jace, who stacked it neatly in the cabinet with the casual grace of someone who'd done it a hundred times.

"Thank you," she said, meaning more than just the omelets.

He leaned against the counter, crossing his arms with a satisfied smirk. "Someone had to save us from the culinary tragedy that is Raisin Bran."

"That Raisin Bran is a classic."

"That Raisin Bran is sad."

"It's name brand!"

"It's a cry for help."

She tossed the dish towel at him. He caught it, grinning, and she turned to leave the kitchen. "Come with me. There's something I want to show you. Something very personal and private that I've never shown anyone else."

That got his attention. He closed the distance between them in two easy steps, slipped his arms around her waist, and pulled her close.

"You mean there's something I *haven't* seen?" he teased, voice low and suggestive.

Spencer rolled her eyes, but she was smiling. "Not *that* kind of private."

She led him down the hall to the last door on the right. Her fingers hesitated briefly on the knob before she pushed it open.

Sunlight filtered through the window, catching on floating specks of dust. The room smelled like paper and faint lavender, filled with the soft chaos of a life in motion. Books lined two walls, some stacked, some shelved, all loved. The desk was massive, well-worn, covered in scattered pages, pens, sticky notes, and a half-empty mug of cold tea.

Jace stepped inside and gave a low whistle. "This room is huge. You could fit a king-size bed in here easy."

Spencer raised a brow. "Really, Jace? You expect me to give up my writing and research space because *you* don't like the size of my bed?"

"It's not comfortable to sleep in."

She smirked. "As if we've been doing much *sleeping* in it anyway."

He grinned, unbothered. "Fair point."

He wandered further in, touching nothing but taking everything in—her world, laid bare. The chaos, the order, the stillness.

Spencer walked to the desk and opened a large folder. "These were Andi's," she said, carefully laying out the contents—several old posters. Some Inferno. Some Jace solo. All vintage, all familiar.

He bent closer, noticing the notes in the margins.

"I labeled them," she said softly. "After she died. When I took them down, I wrote where they'd been in our dorm room. 'Closet door.' 'Framed on nightstand.' 'Above desk.' I guess I just... I don't know. I didn't want to forget."

He picked up one, his younger self grinning out from a magazine fold-out. "This is wild."

Then he paused, pulling out a larger one—creased, wrinkled, clearly once ripped into four pieces, and taped back together.

"Yikes," he said, half-laughing. "What did I do to piss her off?"

Spencer stepped beside him, her smile gone. "I don't know. She never told me. One day it was on the wall above her bed. The next, it wasn't. I asked, and she just said she'd outgrown it."

She hesitated, then added, "After she died, I found it shoved in the back of her closet. Folded. No notes. No explanation. Just... this."

Jace stared at it for a moment, thumb brushing along one of the old tape seams.

"She didn't throw it away," he said quietly.

"No," Spencer whispered. "She just couldn't look at it anymore."

The silence that followed pressed heavy between them.

Jace gently returned the torn poster to the folder, careful with the brittle tape seams. As he closed it, his gaze drifted to the corner of the room.

There, just to the left of the bookcase, sat a medium-sized cardboard box. Not hidden. Not displayed. Just... waiting.

He nodded toward it. "What's that?"

Spencer followed his eyes—and her whole body shifted. Her spine straightened. Her arms crossed without thinking, a shield pulled up from nowhere.

"That's the box from Andi's dad," she said softly. "It came the week before Thanksgiving. Nora forwarded it from her office."

He looked at it again, then back at her. "You haven't opened it?"

She shook her head. "I couldn't. I—I know it's just paper and ink and old photos, but... I wasn't ready." Her voice caught. "I was afraid to open it alone."

Jace stepped closer, his expression gentle now. "You aren't alone anymore."

A pause.

"Do you want to open it?"

Spencer didn't speak for a moment. She just stared at the box, as if trying to decide whether it might burn her if she touched it. Then slowly—hesitantly—she nodded.

"Okay," she whispered. "Yeah. I think I need to."

They moved to the floor in front of the bookcase, where there was enough space to sit side by side. Jace waited silently as she reached for the box and pulled it into her lap. Her hands trembled a little as she sliced through the packing tape.

Inside, layers of tissue and aged paper. A bundle of Polaroids held together by a faded pink ribbon. A small zippered pouch. Three composition notebooks, worn at the corners. A spiral-bound sketchpad.

Spencer pulled out the first journal, her fingers brushing the edge like it might crack open a ghost. She opened to a random page. Skimmed. Andi's voice. Andi's handwriting. Jokes about a professor who talked too loud. A bad cup of coffee. A sketch of a lopsided heart.

Then another page, folded once. She opened it carefully.

She read. And kept reading.

The color drained from her face.

When she finally closed the journal, her knuckles were white around it.

"Spencer—?" Jace began.

"Don't," she said, barely above a whisper.

He stayed quiet, waiting.

Her voice came halting, like each word cost her something. "She tore the poster down after the last time. After he hurt her again. She was fourteen. She never told me. She didn't want anyone looking at her—not even you. Not even a picture of you." Spencer swallowed hard. "She couldn't tear him, so she tore you."

Jace searched her face, but nothing he could say felt right.

Tears slid down her cheeks. "How can I be with you, when she loved you and it hurt her to even look at you?"

"Spencer—"

"Please," she said, stepping back. "Don't."

She clutched the journal like it might hold her together. "I think you should go," she said, voice low and unsteady. "Not because I want you to... but if I stay, it feels like I'm betraying her."

He froze. "Spence—no." He shook his head, stepping closer. "You can't do this. We've fought through worse. Whatever's in that journal, whatever it makes you feel, it doesn't erase us."

Her grip tightened. "You don't understand—"

"Then make me understand." His voice cracked, raw with urgency. "Tell me what you need. Tell me how to fix it. But don't just—" He broke off, exhaling hard. "Don't just push me out."

Her eyes filled. "It's not about fixing it. This isn't something you can fight. Every time I look at you right now, I see what she couldn't look at. And I can't..." Her throat worked. "I can't carry both."

He searched her face, desperate for some opening. "Spence, I love you. I'm not walking away without a fight."

"You can't fight this," she whispered. "Not without making me feel like I'm choosing you over her."

That landed like a stone between them. His shoulders sagged, the fight draining even as his eyes stayed locked on hers.

After a long moment, he nodded once, slow. "I'll go," he said quietly. "But not because I believe we're over. I'll go because you're asking me to—and I love you enough to give you what you think you need."

He disappeared into the bedroom. The sound of a zipper. A bag hitting the floor. When he came back, he stopped at the doorway, then crossed to her. His hand cupped her cheek, thumb brushing away a tear. He pressed his lips to her temple, lingering like he could memorize the feel of her.

"I'll wait for you," he murmured. "I'll wait until your heart is ready to choose me. To choose us."

Her flinch was small, but it was enough. "Don't," she whispered. "Please... don't wait. You deserve more than I can give you."

For a long moment, they stood there—her eyes red and shining, his holding everything he couldn't say.

"I'll never forget you," he said. "And I hope you don't forget us."

He stepped back, let his hand fall, and turned away.

And she... she didn't stop him. She just sank to the floor, curling in on herself as the sobs came, quiet at first, then breaking open. Tears for her past. For her future.

For the life she would never have.

Chapter
Twenty-Nine

♥

*E*aton Rapids, Michigan

The kettle began to whistle just as the phone rang.

Spencer padded barefoot across the kitchen, cardigan wrapped tight, the cold from the tile seeping into her bones. Outside, the backyard lay buried under a fresh blanket of snow, untouched since Sunday. She hadn't shoveled. She hadn't wanted to. She hadn't even wanted to leave the house.

She silenced the kettle and reached for the cordless just as the answering machine clicked on.

Beep.

"Spencer. It's Nora. Pick up the damn phone."

She did. "Morning."

"You got six nominations." No greeting, just Nora's voice buzzing with the kind of excitement Spencer used to feel in her own veins. "Six, Spencer. Best Picture. Actress. Actor. Director. Adapted Screenplay. And, drumroll please, Original Song."

Spencer stared out the window, her breath caught somewhere between her ribs. "The song?"

"Your name is everywhere this morning. Everywhere."

She leaned against the counter. Her tea sat forgotten on the stove. "I don't even know what to say."

"That's a first."

Nora's tone softened. "Spence. This is huge."

"I hate it when you call me Spence."

"Who cares what I call you? You're going to the Oscars. You should be proud."

"I am," she said automatically. "I just... wasn't expecting it."

"Uh-huh. Speaking of expectations, how are those back matter revisions coming for the March release?"

Spencer closed her eyes. "Soon. You'll have them soon."

"You've been saying that since Christmas."

Silence stretched.

Then Nora's voice shifted, quieter but firmer. "Look. I've let it go long enough. You either need to call him or forget him, but you can't keep doing this halfway thing. You cannot let a broken heart ruin your career."

Spencer kept her gaze on the thin curl of steam rising from the kettle. Her throat felt tight enough to close.

What she didn't say, what she couldn't say, was that she hadn't just missed her deadline. She hadn't touched her keyboard since Jace left. Because her words, like her heart, had gone with him.

"I should go," she murmured.

"Spencer—"

"Thanks for calling, Nora. Really."

She clicked the phone off, set it down, and poured the tea. Her hand shook just enough to make the spoon rattle against the cup.

Her cell beeped. A text from Nora:

You will be at the Oscar ceremony, won't you?

Spencer's stomach tightened.

Nashville. Lower Broadway. Country music drifting from open doors. And Jace's voice in her ear:

If the song is nominated for a major award, I'll sing at the ceremony. For you. Because you asked me to.

He would sing because she asked him to. He left because she asked him to. Would he come back if she asked him to?

She pushed the thought aside. She could not dwell on it. If she did, she might call him, just to find out.

Chapter Thirty

os Angeles, California

L The blinds were drawn. The TV was muted, frozen on a
paused frame of a PlayStation game he hadn't touched in over an
hour. The controller sat in his lap. Wrinkled pajama bottoms, a hoodie
zipped halfway, and hair slick at the roots from days without washing completed the picture. The air was heavy with stale takeout and
something else, something that smelled like defeat.

He hadn't checked his phone. Hadn't opened his email. Not since
he turned off the news the moment the nominations were read.

But he heard them whispering.

Low voices from the kitchen, just beyond the wall. His mother and
sister, trading the kind of whispers that made his skin prickle.

"I don't want to tell him. You tell him."

"No way. You saw him yesterday. I'm not poking that bear."

"Someone needs to tell him."

His voice cut through the quiet like a snapped guitar string.

"I already know, okay?"

Carol Anne and Heather froze.

He was in the hallway now, half-hidden in shadow, a Gatorade bottle in one hand. His bloodshot eyes didn't blink.

"Six." The word landed hard. "She got six nominations. Including one for that stupid song."

He tipped the bottle back, draining it, then hurled it toward the kitchen wall. It hit with a hollow thud and bounced across the tile.

"Thanks for that, by the way." His voice cracked under the bitterness. "If you hadn't asked me, I wouldn't have recorded it. I could have stayed behind the scenes. Happy. Quiet. Unripped."

His glare locked on Heather.

"You just had to ask me to do that one song."

He dropped into a brittle imitation. "'What could it hurt, Jason? It's not a full album. It's not a tour. You don't even have to see the other guys. This could be fun.'"

A short, joyless laugh scraped out of him. "Yeah. A freakin' blast."

No one spoke.

He turned away, his footsteps heavy on the hardwood.

By the time Carol Anne and Heather followed, he was back on the couch, eyes fixed on nothing. The controller was in his lap again, unmoving. His thumb twitched over the analog stick, but the screen stayed frozen.

Carol Anne's voice was gentle. "It's an incredible accomplishment. A song you helped write and record, nominated for an Oscar. After all this time away from the spotlight, it proves they were wrong about you. You are more talented than they ever believed."

"You should be celebrating," Heather said, wrinkling her nose at the sour air. "Not wallowing in this mess."

"What's the point? She's not here."

Heather set down the coffee she had brought him and pushed aside some unopened mail. "You should call her."

"She made her choice. She chose grief. She chose guilt. She didn't choose me."

Heather crossed her arms. "So now what? You sit here in your own stink until the ceremony?"

He shrugged. "Why stop at the ceremony? I might as well stay here, killing zombies in Resident Evil for the rest of my life. I'm too broken for anything else."

Carol Anne sat on the armrest and ran her fingers through his hair before wiping them on her jeans.

"You're not broken," she said softly. "You're bruised. That's all."

"Doesn't feel like it."

Heather muttered, "You smell more broken than bruised."

The corner of his mouth twitched. Barely. But it was something.

"She's probably out celebrating," he said quietly. "Maybe halfway through her next book. Probably hasn't even noticed I wasn't there."

Carol Anne and Heather exchanged a look.

He caught it. "What?"

Heather hesitated. "You really haven't heard?"

His eyes narrowed. "Heard what?"

"She's not writing," Heather said.

He blinked, the words taking a moment to land.

Heather went on. "The release is on hold. The publisher's close to pulling the plug. People says she's missed deadlines and broken her contract."

His voice was barely a whisper. "Why?"

Carol Anne spoke gently. "She's miserable too, sweetheart. She's not celebrating. She's unraveling."

There was a beat of silence. Then Heather asked, "So... are you going to the ceremony?"

He looked at her like she had just suggested walking barefoot over broken glass. "Why would I?"

Carol Anne tilted her head. "Because it's a once-in-a-lifetime moment? Because you deserve to be there?"

His jaw tightened. "Because I promised her I'd sing if the song was nominated." His mouth curved into something that wasn't quite a smile. " And I've never been able to say no to beautiful women and their stupid requests."

Carol Anne frowned. "What does that mean?"

"It means," he said bitterly, "I'm going to the blasted Oscars."

Heather let out a sharp breath and turned toward the stairs. "At least take a shower first. You smell worse than the La Brea Tar Pits in July."

Carol Anne didn't disagree.

Jace gave a dry smirk. "Thanks for the support."

"I'm your sister, not your bra," Heather said. "And right now, you need more help than even eighteen hours could give you."

Chapter Thirty-One

♥

The car had been parked for three full minutes. Long enough for the heat to fade from the vents. Long enough for the driver to glance back twice.

She was already there.

Spencer.

Framed by camera flashes and elegance, she stood between Jake Gyllenhaal and Amy Adams, her smile dazzling for the cameras, her posture as poised as ever, though he caught the slight sag in her shoulders and the restless sway that told him she wanted to be anywhere else. The black dress hugged her curves without clinging, understated in the way that made every tabloid stylist swoon. Diamond clips caught the light in her auburn waves, pulling them gently back from her face.

She looked breathtaking.

Jace sat with one hand clenched around the Oscar invitation in his lap and the other gripping the door handle. Every instinct told him to stay in the car. Or better yet, tell the driver to pull away, to lose himself somewhere in the Los Angeles night.

But she had asked him once to sing her words.

And he had promised.

The driver shifted in his seat. "Mr. Rose, there are others waiting for this spot."

Jace swallowed hard, glanced once more through the tinted window, and let out a breath that felt like stepping off a ledge.

"Right. Yeah."

The door opened.

The crowd recognized him instantly.

"Jace! Over here!"

"Jace Rose, is the song going to win tonight?"

"Can we get a shot?"

He waved. Smiled. Stepped onto the carpet like it didn't feel like glass beneath his feet.

And then—

She turned.

Their eyes locked.

A full second passed. Then another. Then three.

The cameras still flashed. The interviews carried on. But for him, the noise dropped away.

Spencer Callahan. Angie.

The woman who had broken his heart and still carried it.

She didn't smile. Didn't look away.

She lifted her hand.

Not in greeting. Not in dismissal.

An invitation.

A silent, graceful plea—*come stand with us.*

Come stand with me.

He stepped forward.

And the world exhaled.

□□□

She wasn't looking for him.

Not at all.

At least, that's what she told herself.

She was smiling for the cameras, standing with Amy on one side and Jake on the other, Zach a half-step behind them, all four of them fielding questions about *Fighting Gravity*. The kind she could answer in her sleep — about themes and characters, about the transition from page to screen, about what it meant to be nominated.

She had it down to muscle memory. Smile. Speak clearly. Make eye contact. Smile again.

And then the crowd shifted.

"Jace! Over here!"

"Jace Rose, is the song going to win tonight?"

"Jace! Are you and Spencer Callahan a couple?"

Her smile faltered.

Only a little. Just enough for her to feel it. The cameras wouldn't catch it. She hoped.

She didn't turn.

Didn't need to.

She felt him.

The pull of his presence. The hum under her skin. The way her heartbeat tripped over itself before racing to catch up.

He was here.

And he wasn't moving.

The others kept smiling, kept posing. But Zach leaned in, his voice low. "He's waiting for you to tell him it's okay."

Okay.

Was it?

If she let him stand beside her, walk with her, breathe the same air... could she pretend none of it mattered? That she hadn't pushed him away, watching him carry her heart into the snow?

She was an author, not an actress. Could she fake that much?

She didn't answer the question.

Her hand lifted on instinct — soft, slow, angled just enough to the side. An invitation.

Across the carpet, his eyes found hers.

And then he smiled.

He crossed to her, careful but sure, and took the offered hand. The cameras erupted.

They posed. They laughed. They answered questions together. And somewhere in the middle of it, she leaned in and whispered, "You smell amazing."

He didn't miss a beat. "You look amazing."

Her gaze caught his, and she saw it there — the ache, the hope, the flicker of before.

For one dizzy, impossible moment, she thought he was going to kiss her.

Right there. In front of the whole world.

But the moment broke.

Handlers waved. Publicists signaled.

They were ushered forward, hands slipping apart too soon.

Inside the theater, the lights dimmed. Their seats were waiting. The ceremony was about to begin.

And Spencer reminded herself she was here for the film. For the words. For the dream that had outlived the pain.

She smiled for the cameras one last time.

And told herself the tears in her eyes were joy. And hope. And disbelief.

Not heartbreak.

Not this time.

Chapter Thirty-Two

♥

The lights dimmed again.

Spencer straightened in her seat, her hands resting over the silver clutch in her lap. She had been doing her best not to fidget, not to think about what might be coming. Jace had been quiet beside her for most of the ceremony—offering the occasional smile, a whispered comment or two, but mostly watching in stillness.

Somewhere between one segment and the next, he had slipped away.

She hadn't noticed at first. Not until the seat beside her was empty, and the memory from Nashville hit her like a whisper — *If the song is nominated for a major award, I'll sing at the ceremony. For you. Because you asked me to.*

The presenter stepped up to the mic.

"Here to perform *Back From the Edge*, the Oscar-nominated song from *Fighting Gravity*—a haunting ballad that captures the feeling of a life on the verge of collapse, and the steady hand of love and friendship that pulls it back from the edge—please welcome Jace Rose."

The breath caught in her chest.

Stage lights rose.

And there he was.

No orchestra. No production. Just a stool, a guitar, and the man who used to hold her heart like it was made of glass.

He sat center stage, head bowed slightly, guitar resting against his knee. He'd shed the tuxedo jacket, undone the bowtie, left his shirt collar open. His sleeves were rolled to his forearms, just enough to break the red carpet illusion. He didn't look like a celebrity now.

He looked like Jace. Her Jace. The man it was killing her to live without.

He adjusted the mic, nodded once, and began to play.

The first chord rang out—low and spare, but steady. Then another. And then—

He sang.

Fading in the silence, Drowning in the weight of days, Counting cracks along the ceiling, Watching time just slip away.

His voice wasn't polished. Wasn't perfect.

It was *honest.*

The guitar carried him into the next verse, soft and unhurried.

Every mirror told a story I was too afraid to hear, Every smile was borrowed, Every heartbeat laced with fear.

Spencer's throat tightened.

But then you reached through the shadows, Laid your hand against my skin, You didn't beg me to be stronger You just let the light come in.

You didn't say that it'd be easy, You just stayed until I could breathe .You pulled me back from the edge, When all I wanted was to leave.

The room had gone still.

No one moved. No one whispered.

He let the last chord of the chorus fade before starting again.

Slept beneath the thunder, Let the silence scream me blind, Every step was hollow, Every promise left behind.

His voice broke slightly—not on pitch, just on feeling.

Held me like an answer To a question I forgot, You believed before I did That I was worth a lot.

Spencer's eyes burned. She didn't blink.

You reached through the shadows, Laid your hand against my skin, Didn't push or ask for answers You just let the light come in.

You didn't say that I'd be better, You just stayed so I could see, You pulled me back from the edge, When all I wanted was to leave.

The second chorus drifted into the bridge.

Jace leaned into the mic.

Lower. Slower. Closer.

You didn't fix the pieces, You just helped me pick them up. You never claimed to save me...

And then...

He looked up.

Right at her.

Her Jace. The man she had let go, even when it broke her.

You just loved me hard enough.

She couldn't breathe.

Couldn't look away.

And somewhere between that lyric and the final chorus, she realized she was crying.

She reached for her clutch, fumbling, but Amy was quicker. The folded tissue was in her hand before she could ask. Still smiling for the cameras, Amy leaned in and whispered, "That man might be worth ruining your mascara on."

Spencer laughed softly, the sound catching in her throat.

Then came the final chorus.

You reached through the shadows, Held on when I slipped away, You stayed quiet in the chaos Till I had the words to say.

You didn't ask me for redemption,You just stayed and set me free.You pulled me back from the edgeNow I finally want to be.

He let the last chord ring out.

Then silence.

No bow. No smile.

Just Jace, eyes down, hands still.

Then the lights dimmed.

And the applause came—wave after wave, rolling through the room like thunder.

Somewhere along the way, she had stopped hearing him sing about Cassie and Max. She had only heard him singing about them. Spencer and Jace.

Spencer clapped with everyone else, her smile fixed for the cameras. But inside, her heart was still catching up to the truth she couldn't outrun.

The song had been for her. Every word. Every note.

And no matter how far apart they were, he was still her Jace.

Spencer clapped because that's what was expected.

But her heart hadn't stopped shaking.

Chapter
Thirty-Three

♥

He made his way back to the auditorium, trying not to look for her. He'd stared at her enough throughout the performance. He'd seen the music reach her heart, and knew keeping his promise had been the right thing. Even if she didn't go home with him, even if he never held her in his arms again, the memory of Spencer smiling through her tears would be enough for him.

The night could have ended after that moment, and Jace would have gone home feeling like a winner.

Now, twenty minutes later, Spencer's hand was still resting near his. Not holding. Just... there. It took every ounce of his strength not to grasp it.

Then the lights shifted again.

The announcer's voice came through the speakers:

"Ladies and gentlemen, please welcome... Bette Midler."

The crowd applauded as Bette stepped into view—bright, joyful, commanding the room with a single look. She stood at the mic in a floor-length gown, beaming like she knew every secret in the world.

"Good evening. You know, the beautiful thing about music in film is that it stays with us... long after the credits roll. It tucks into our hearts, wraps itself around a memory, and refuses to let go."

She let the words land, then continued.

"The songs nominated tonight gave voice to love, to grief, to hope... and to survival. Here are the nominees for Best Original Song."

The screen lit up behind her, five titles appearing one by one. A brief clip played with each, no more than ten seconds, just enough to stir the audience.

Bette read them aloud with reverence and ease, adding a little warmth to each name as if she personally knew the people behind them.

"*Back From the Edge*, from *Fighting Gravity*. Words by Spencer Callahan and Jace Rose. Music by Jace Rose."

The shot cut to Spencer and Jace. He smiled politely. She nodded once, fingers tightening on the clutch in her lap.

"*Falling Through Stars*, from *Skyline Dreams*. Written by Madison Jayne and Per Nilson."

A flash of Madison in the crowd, her expression poised and camera-ready.

"*My Own Hallelujah*, from *Hearts on Fire*. Written by Noah Sidney and Tessa Hart."

Tessa blew a kiss toward the stage. Noah didn't move.

"*Paint the Silence*, from *The Girl in Room 27*. Written by Sofia Lark and Darren Tse."

A stark, haunting piano note lingered as the title faded.

"*After the Storm*, from *Seasons of Wind*. Written by Greta Holloway and Lin-Manuel Rivera."

Lush orchestration played behind sweeping shots of snow and bare trees.

The screen went dark again.

Bette smiled, opening the envelope with graceful flair.

She glanced at the card, then looked out over the audience.

"And the Oscar goes to..."

A sparkle lit her expression.

"*Back From the Edge*, from *Fighting Gravity*."

The room erupted into applause.

It hit like a wave, distant at first, then suddenly loud and bright and very, very real.

Jace exhaled. He didn't know he had been holding his breath.

Beside him, Spencer turned. Their eyes met.

Neither said a word.

He stood first, reaching for her hand.

She rose with him.

The cameras followed as they stepped into the aisle. Polite clapping turned into cheers from the deeper rows. Somewhere on the balcony, someone whooped loud enough to make Spencer laugh, just once, soft, and surprised.

At the base of the stairs, she paused.

He stopped with her.

She looked up at him, not as Spencer Callahan the writer, or Angie Smith who once loved him, but as the woman who had just won an Academy Award with him. And, in the deepest corner of her heart, still as his.

Then she slipped her arm through his.

They walked up the stairs together.

Side by side.

Not as a couple. Not as a spectacle.

Just as partners. Partners in art, in pain, in healing.

The applause swelled again as they reached the podium.

A stagehand handed over the gold statues, one for each of them. Jace accepted his with a slight bow of the head. Spencer did the same.

She stepped toward the mic.

"Wow," she said softly, her eyes still on the award in her hand. "This is... unreal. I don't even know what to say."

Then she looked up at him.

Just for a second.

The smile she gave him was small. Soft. Almost shy.

Then she turned to the audience, then to the camera.

"This," she said, lifting the statuette just slightly, "is for my eleventh grade creative writing teacher, Mr. Henderson, who told me my attempts at poetry were nothing but chaotic drivel and would never win any awards. Never say never, Mr. H.!"

The room laughed. Warmly. Appreciatively.

Jace smiled, too, even though his chest felt tight.

The laughter faded into another round of applause, short and sincere.

Spencer cleared her throat, just enough to steady herself. "Thank you to the Academy, of course. To the incredible team behind *Fighting Gravity*—Zach, Amy, Jake, everyone who brought this story to life with so much care. To Jace," she glanced at him briefly, smiling, "for writing the music that haunts my dreams. Thank you to my readers, who have stuck with me through stories that weren't always easy. And to my agent Nora—who's probably glaring at me right now for forgetting to mention her first."

A ripple of chuckles moved through the front rows. Spencer smiled again, easier this time.

She glanced once more toward Jace, then stepped back from the mic.

He didn't move at first.

Not until she turned and gave him the faintest nod—permission or invitation, he couldn't tell which.

He stepped forward.

Oscar still in hand.

Microphone waiting.

The crowd quieted.

And all he could think, as the silence stretched out in front of him, was how much easier it had been to sing.

"Thank you," he began, voice low but clear. "To the Academy. To the team at Westlight. To the cast and crew of *Fighting Gravity*—Zach, Amy, Jake... you brought Spencer's story to life with grace and heart."

He paused. Just a breath.

"Thank you to Spencer—for writing the words that gave my music something to live inside."

Out of the corner of his eye, she didn't move.

He looked toward the front row.

"Thank you to my mom and my sister—for reminding me that just because I stopped singing... didn't mean I stopped having something to say."

Another beat.

Then his gaze lifted—not to Spencer, not to the crowd.

To the camera.

Direct. Intentional.

"Angie," he said quietly. "Thank you for loving me hard enough to show me how to live again."

His grip tightened on the statue in his hand.

"I'll never forget our time together. And I'll always protect those memories... even if they're all I have left."

He paused, just long enough to steady his voice.

Then, softer, the words barely above a whisper, "I will always love you."

The orchestra swelled behind him, the cue clear.

Jace stepped back, nodding once.

Then he turned toward Spencer, extended his hand.

She stared at him—stunned, maybe, but not unsure. And somewhere inside, her heart answered him even if her lips did not.

Their fingers met.

He led her offstage as the music rose around them.

And neither of them looked back.

Chapter Thirty-Four

♥

S pencer sat perfectly still, statue resting in her lap, fingers curled tight around the base.

It had been nearly forty minutes since they had walked off stage. Forty minutes since he said those words. Since he looked into the camera and told the world what she hadn't let herself believe he still felt.

Angie, thank you for loving me hard enough to show me how to live again... I'll always protect those memories. Even if they're all I have left. I will always love you.

She hadn't been able to breathe properly since.

Now they sat side by side again, close enough that her arm brushed his every time she shifted. Every inch of her body buzzed with the urge to reach for his hand. To lean just slightly into the warmth of him. To do something—anything—that might let her believe what he said still mattered.

But she didn't move.

Didn't even blink.

Her mind was too full of him. His voice. His words. That impossible truth laid bare beneath stage lights and cameras.

She was so lost in it, she barely registered the applause. The envelope. Alan Rickman onstage, reading names she should have been listening to.

Then—

A kiss. Light, barely there, pressed to her cheek.

"You did it," Jace whispered. His voice was low, awed. Proud. "You won."

Her brows pulled together. "I... what?"

The crowd was cheering. Clapping.

Her name.

They were saying her name.

She blinked hard, glancing at the screen on the stage. Best Adapted Screenplay. And her name being shouted through the auditorium.

Zach was already rising to his feet beside her, hand outstretched. Jake stood on her other side.

They each took one of her arms, but she walked on her own.

She climbed the stairs with unsteady grace and took the statue with both hands, accepting the kiss on the cheek from Alan Rickman like it was happening in a dream.

Then she turned to the mic.

She had a speech written. Memorized. Practiced.

She didn't use it.

"I wrote *Fighting Gravity* because of a pain I watched my best friend live through," she said, voice steady but soft, "and then carried for years after her death. I didn't know how to speak that pain. So I gave it to someone else, a girl I named Cassie Freeman. I'd hoped she'd help me heal, but I didn't know she'd lead me here."

She paused, breath catching as she glanced toward the first row.

"I gave Cassie what I thought my friend needed. What I wish she'd had... Max Butler. Everyone needs a Max in their life. Someone who lifts you when you're too tired to stand. Someone who believes in you when the rest of the world stops. For years, I tried to be that person for myself."

Her gaze swept the room.

The crowd believed she was looking at Jake Gyllenhaal, who had so perfectly embodied Max on screen.

But she wasn't.

Her eyes found him. Her Jace.

Her fingers eased around the statue, the tension in her shoulders loosening. A small smile touched her lips—one she hoped he knew was only for him.

"Until I met my own Max... and didn't realize it until I lost him."

The words seemed to hang in the air, the last note of a love song no one knew they'd been hearing.

"This award is for him." Her gaze stayed on him now, watching the way his lips parted, his eyes wide with something that looked like wonder. "For his love. For his understanding. For his support and belief in me. And for the hope that... it's not too late to say I love you."

She gave a single, quiet nod.

"Thank you."

She followed Alan Rickman offstage without looking back. She didn't have to. She could feel his eyes on her, steady and unshaken, with every step she took.

Chapter Thirty-Five

♥

The lights above the press line were still blinding, even after hours of smiling at them. Spencer blinked through the flashbulbs as Wendy Rakowski from *People* stepped closer, recorder in hand, eyes gleaming.

Spencer adjusted the weight of the Oscars in her arms—one for Best Adapted Screenplay, the other for Best Original Song—and gave a tired but genuine smile.

Wendy grinned. "I have to tell you, this is a real honor. You're actually my favorite author. I've been hooked on your work since *Broken by You* came out in 2000."

Spencer's eyes lit. "Seriously? That means a lot. You've been my favorite journalist for years. I may or may not hoard old *People* issues with your red carpet interviews in them."

Wendy laughed. "Okay, now I'm flattered."

She glanced toward the stage where Jake Gyllenhaal was still talking with someone from *Variety*, then leaned in just slightly. "Also... completely off the record, but your version of Max Butler may have ruined dating for me. Jake brought him to life a little too well."

Spencer smirked. "Would you like to meet him?"

Wendy blinked. "Wait, are you serious?"

"I'm pretty sure he'd be flattered," Spencer said, dropping her voice as if sharing the biggest secret. "He's also very single."

Before Wendy could turn into a total fangirl, her tone shifted—more thoughtful now. "So... that speech. I especially loved the part about Max." She hesitated. "Did you really find your Max?"

Spencer's smile wavered. She looked down at the golden statuettes in her arms, their gleam blurred by the tears threatening her lashes.

"I did," she said quietly. "I found him... and I lost him." She met Wendy's eyes with a sad, honest shrug. "And I think it's too late to get him back."

A new voice broke through the crowd.

"Excuse me, Wendy."

Spencer turned.

Jace.

Tuxedo crisp. Hair slightly windswept. Eyes locked on hers like he hadn't looked away all night.

He stepped closer and held out his Oscar. "Would you mind holding this for a second?"

Wendy blinked. "Uh—sure."

She took it, stunned, and before she could say another word, Jace stepped forward.

Closed the distance.

Cupped Spencer's face in both hands.

Whispered, "It's never too late, Spencer."

And kissed her.

Not for the crowd.

Not for the camera.

For her.

The kind of kiss that rewrites the silence and sets fire to every wall she'd tried to build.

Spencer let the Oscars fall—one thudding softly onto the carpet, the other caught midair by someone with faster reflexes—and wrapped her arms around his neck like he was the only solid thing in the room.

When they finally came up for air, her voice trembled.

"Oh, Jace. I love you."

He smiled. That smile.

"It took you long enough," he said simply.

Her laugh was quiet, shaky, still catching on leftover tears.

And then he kissed her again.

Behind them, Wendy let out a breathless, awestruck sigh.

"Now that's my cover story."

Epilogue

♥

Eaton Rapids, Michigan
One Year Later

The house smelled like cardboard, dust, and the faintest trace of lavender from a candle she hadn't lit in months. She hadn't truly lived here in months either—not since the Oscars, not since LA stopped being a stopover and started feeling like home.

She'd only returned in short bursts, long enough to grab clothes, water the plants, and pretend she was still Angie Smith for a weekend. But the truth was, Angie had stopped living here long ago. Now she was packing up the last pieces of that life—pieces better left in memory—so Spencer Callahan could step fully into hers.

Just two more boxes to go.

In two days, she'd be on a flight to LA. Filming started next week. Their first joint project—a Disney-friendly musical loosely based on the play Andi had written in seventh grade. Something about a girl who talked to ghosts and a boy who couldn't sing but somehow saved the world with music.

Spencer wrote the screenplay. Jace wrote the songs.

Her eyes lifted to the wall above the fireplace, catching on the framed *People* magazine cover. March 2006.She and Jace, shoulder to shoulder, caught mid-laugh, faces close in formalwear and joy. Three Oscars between them. One kiss in the flashbulbs.

Across the top, in bold gold letters: **Two Oscars and a Max: Spencer Callahan's Unforgettable Night**

Spencer snorted softly. "Still hate that title."

From the kitchen came his voice, warm and teasing. "I told you—you should've let me write the headline."

"Oh yeah? And what would you have picked?"

He appeared in the doorway, two mugs in hand, leaning there for a beat like he'd been watching her. That grin she still wasn't immune to curved his mouth as he crossed the room.

"I don't know," he said, handing her the coffee, "something honest."

She arched a brow. "Like?"

He brushed a kiss to her temple. "The night the fairytale came true."

Sliding his arms around her waist, he pulled her back against him. "You know I love you, right?"

"Mmm-hmm." She sipped her coffee. "I knew that long before you ever said it."

"So you know I'm not trying to talk you out of anything. But are you sure about this?" His lips lingered at her cheek. "You don't have to sell your house and walk away from being Angie for us to have a future."

"I know." She rested her free hand over his. "But it's time. I need to let Angie go—Andi, too—if I'm going to be ready for a future with you."

Her fingers traced along his knuckles. "Angie lost Andi, and I survived—as Spencer. But Spencer couldn't survive losing you, Jace."

His chin found her shoulder, voice low. "Good thing you're stuck with me, then."

She turned in his arms, searching his face. "Guess it really wasn't too late after all."

His smile deepened. "Not even close."

He kissed her slowly, certain and warm, sealing the promise in a way words never could.

Somewhere beyond the walls of the house, the world was waiting. the set, the music, the story they were about to bring to life together.

But for now, there was just this. Her Jace. Her future. And not a single reason to look back.

Books By Baxter Redman

Flying Without Wings

The Boy Band Saga – Book One

She wasn't looking for love. He wasn't looking for forever.

When publicist Sydney Walsh agrees to work with Synergy, the hottest boy band in the country, she knows it will test her patience—and maybe her heart. Lead singer Joshua Damian is everything she shouldn't want: charming, stubborn, and absolutely off-limits. But the music industry has its own rhythm, and sometimes love finds a way to change the beat.

Everything Changes

The Boy Band Saga – Book Two

COMING SOON

Publicist Sydney Walsh thought she could keep her heart and her career separate. But when her secret romance with pop star Joshua Damian collides with manipulative bosses, backstage betrayals, and the relentless spotlight, she is forced to face the truth: in this world, nothing stays hidden forever.

From high-energy tour stops to quiet moments that change everything, Sydney and Josh's love will be tested in ways neither saw coming. One wrong move could cost them everything, but one leap of faith might just rewrite their future.

A Thousand Miles
COMING SOON

Once an Olympic champion, Layla Trent thought she understood pressure. She was wrong.

When cancer forces her into the public eye and a documentary crew follows her into surgery, survival becomes a performance she never agreed to rehearse. Then her ex-husband walks back into her life, carrying unfinished love, old wounds, and impossible choices.

A Thousand Miles is a raw, intimate story about illness, fame, and the terrifying courage it takes to choose yourself—and love again.

About the Author

Baxter Redman writes contemporary romance filled with heart, humor, and characters you can't help but root for. A lifelong fan of boy bands and pop culture, Baxter blends backstage drama with real-world emotion, creating stories that are as swoony as they are unforgettable.

When she's not writing, Baxter can usually be found with coffee in hand, planning the next book playlist, or rewatching her favorite 90s music videos "for research." She is the mother of three adult sons. She makes her home in Michigan with her three dogs and her high school sweetheart husband, who happily supports her boy band obsession, secure in the knowledge that his are the only lips she kisses goodnight.

www.ingramcontent.com/pod-product-compliance
Lightning Source LLC
Chambersburg PA
CBHW050841180626
46814CB00007B/2573